Books in

The Human-Hybrid Project

series:

The Mirror Cracks

The Mirror Cracks

Farley L. Dunn

THREE SKILLET

Published in Fort Worth, Texas

 THREE SKILLET

www.ThreeSkilletPublishing.com

Three Skillet Publishing
PO Box 162194
Fort Worth, Texas 76161

ISBN: 978-1-943189-93-9

First Printing July 2021/Printed in the USA

The Mirror Cracks

— Book 3 —

The Human-Hybrid Project

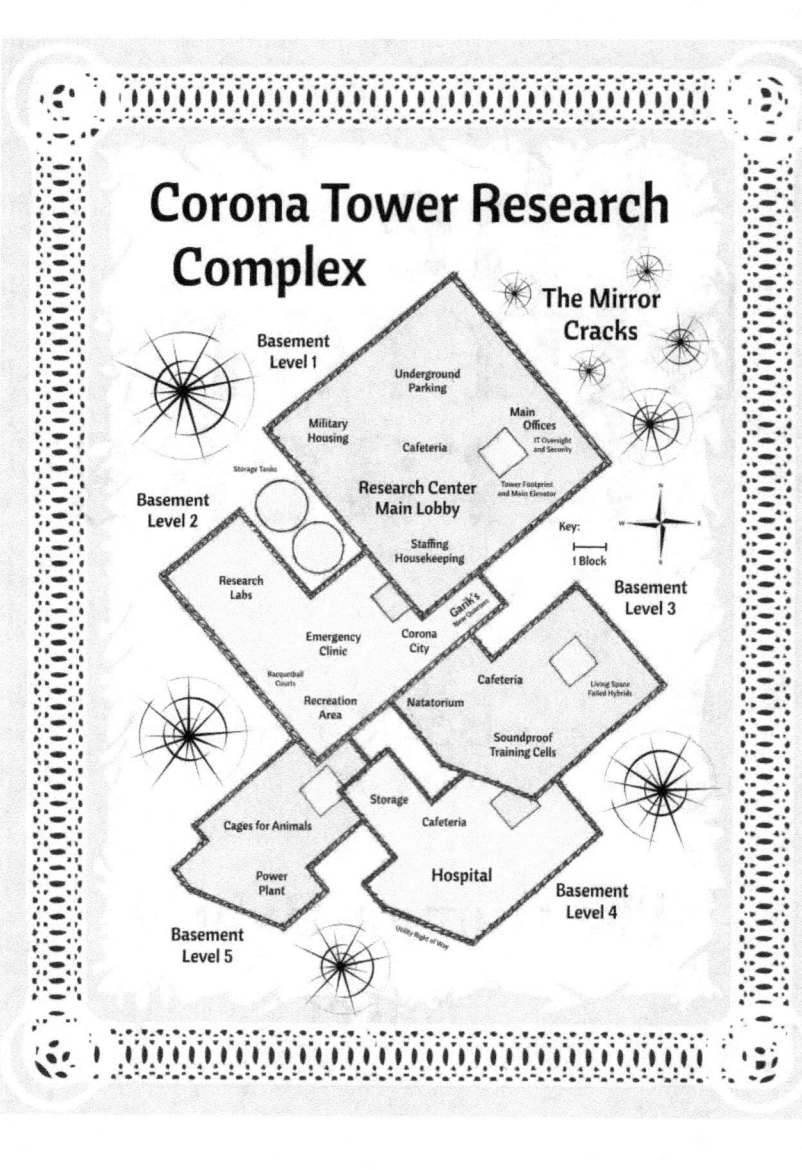

Corona Tower Research Complex

The Mirror Cracks

Basement Level 1

Basement Level 2

Basement Level 3

Basement Level 4

Basement Level 5

Underground Parking

Military Housing

Cafeteria

Main Offices

IT Oversight and Security

Storage Tanks

Research Center Main Lobby

Tower Footprint and Main Elevator

Staffing Housekeeping

Research Labs

Garik's New Quarters

Emergency Clinic

Corona City

Racquetball Courts

Recreation Area

Natatorium

Cafeteria

Living Space Failed Hybrids

Soundproof Training Cells

Storage

Cages for Animals

Cafeteria

Power Plant

Hospital

Utility Right of Way

Key:

1 Block

— I —

arik Shayk pressed his shoulders into the iron bar, his leg muscles quivering, uncertain now if the extra weight his spotter had added at the ends was wise.

"I've got you." The shadows of his spotter's arms danced across the floor.

"Are you—" Garik strained, groaning with the effort of lifting the bar, and he yelped, "—sure?"

"Yes, sure. Don't be soft. You can do this. What's a few extra pounds? Such a tiny increase. Up, softie! Success is yours." The spotter tapped the undersides of Garik's arms, then harder when he failed to get an adequate response.

"So you say." Garik gave a final push, felt the bar slip into the forks on the top of the stand, and he leaned over, his hands on his knees, his legs quivering and barely able to breathe. Sweat coated his face and burned his eyes.

"Your towel." The towel appeared in front of him.

Garik opened it, pressed it to his face, and almost immediately jerked it away, spitting. "Aw, Christian, you've been shedding all over my towel again. Gross! What did you say your gene splice was with? Llama?"

"Wolfhound. I'm sorry. We shed."

To Garik's way of thinking, the man didn't sound sorry at all. He thought back four weeks to the reason he was working out with Christian at all.

"LEAH, GOOD morning. May I come in?" Garik was at the hospital on Basement Level 4. He was here to see Dr. Jimenez.

His passkey only allowed him access to the cafeteria on Level 1, his quarters on Level 2, and the training center on Level 3. Van Hermoso, his occupational therapist, had been doubtful about his request to visit the hospital.

"You do know I was tested yesterday, right?" Garik was very polite, making sure he appealed to Van's compassionate side. He was also very sore, but he didn't mention that. He certainly didn't want to offend him. If he did, his plan would be scorched before it had time to rise in the oven.

"Of course. I was there." Garik had caught Van at breakfast, and the pock-faced fitness nut was spooning shredded wheat into his mouth, a substantial spoonful at a time. He talked around his food. "What does that have to do with visiting the hospital? The emergency clinic can be accessed by your key. Go there to get what you need."

Ouch! After the tests he had been put through the day before—and his supreme failure—Garik knew he was beneath anyone's notice. This was proof.

"I, um, well—" and Garik put a quiver into his bottom lip, "—see, I lied to Dr. Jamie. I'm sorry, Van. I couldn't help myself, and I want to apologize."

"You *lied* to him?" Van grinned. "You freakin' *lied* to the man? That's rich. He's gonna roast you. What did you lie to him about?" He took another wheat biscuit and began to shred it into his bowl.

"I said I was doing my best, and really, I was just tired and wanted to go back to my room." Garik tried a half smile, the sort that sometimes worked as an apology at school when he didn't have his homework. "You know how it is."

"No, I don't know." He took his spoon and dipped up another chunk of shredded wheat and pushed the entire thing in his mouth. Over the food, he said, "I don't get tired. I get fit. But I want to see you get ripped apart by the doctor."

That had gotten Garik to Level 4, and now he had Nurse Ratchett, his nickname for Leah Fortinier, Dr. Jimenez's personal nurse, to navigate.

"Yes, Garik, come in. I see your hair is improving. Yesterday, well, that was a shame. We all had such high hopes for you. I'm sure the research center will find a good place for you." She smiled, as bright and sunshiny as ever, even as she told him she now knew he was a loser, and she was disappointed, but not too much to continue with her everyday life bringing new human hybrids into existence, either with or without their consent.

"That's just it, Leah. You see, I need to apologize to Dr. Jamie." He smiled his apologetic smile. "I know I let him down, and it didn't have to happen that way. I know he expected more of me, and I failed to give it to him. I can be so much better. I was certain I could fool everyone into going easy on me, and now I know you saw through me. I've learned my lesson, and I'll give a hundred percent if you'll let me try again."

"Oh, this is a change of attitude." Leah smiled, very pleased. "I'm sure Dr. Jamie would like to hear what you have to say. Please wait right over there." She pointed to a set of two chairs with vinyl seats and backs, the sort that were sticky to sit on and worse to stand out of.

Garik smiled, said, "Thank you, Leah. I appreciate

your help," and he gently lowered himself into the chair farthest from the door, so that anyone else who came in could have the best seat.

"SO, MR., UM—" Dr. Jimenez paused, undecided on the proper form of Garik's name to use. He looked up with a half-hearted smile and chose to use neither his first name nor his last. "Yes, my boy. What can I help you with?"

Leah had been very insistent over the intercom that *the young man from yesterday* was here to *apologize to you, Dr. Jamie.* Now, he didn't seem to know if he should call him Mr. Out-the-Door Shayk or good-friend Garik. Garik was amused, but not enough to risk his plan.

First, he repeated his apology, using his most contrite face, the one most apt to get him out of sticky situations in the past, and then he moved on to the heart of his proposal.

"See, Dr. Jamie—" he knew the man would warm up to Garik using his first name, "—I know if I trained more, really put my best effort into being all you want me to be, I can be a success. I want to make you proud of your efforts with me. The thing is, I've never done this. I've been going it alone, and I feel like I'm flailing around. I'm hopeless at this sort of thing."

"Hopeless, huh?" Dr. Jimenez leaned back in his chair. "Flailing, you say? Do you have any ideas on how you plan to change that?"

"I'm glad you asked, Dr. Jamie, because I've been thinking about that. I need a trainer—"

"You already have Van and that, um, Devon boy. Have you asked them?"

"Here's how I see it, Dr. Jamie." Garik saw the man's expression warm up every time he used his first name. "I need someone like me, someone who's had the same thing done to them that you guys are trying with me."

"I don't see how—" The doctor leaned forward, frowning, and Garik interrupted him.

"That's just it, Dr. Jamie." Bingo! The man smiled. "If there was someone who was DNA adjusted for exactly what you're looking for in me, then they would know exactly how to train me."

"I, um, think I see what you mean."

"Is there someone, Dr. Jamie? I hope so. I so want to be everything you hope I can be." Garik put his desperate face on.

"Well, there is one man, but he's scheduled to be reassigned. I don't know if it's too late—"

"Will you try, please?" He was talking about Christian. He had to be, because that was Garik's plan, to save Christian from being reassigned to Basement Level 5 where he would be genetically harvested for research. There was no reason to grovel like this, otherwise.

And that was why Garik Shayk was lifting weights he didn't want to lift, to give the research team a reason to value Christian Maguire's presence in the human-hybrid project and keep him on until Jantzen Hefferly could concoct a plan to rescue the failed hybrid from being terminated.

In the meantime, Christian knelt by the pool with a whistle in his mouth. Garik could now do far more than twelve laps fully clothed with a loaded pack, but they were working on underwater breathing skills. The pool was a full fifty meters, and Garik was on his fifth lap without coming up for air. With four weeks of practice, he was amazed how easy it had become. At the end of his fifth lap, he heard Christian blow the whistle, and he paused, looked up at his workout trainer, waved at the wavering image he could see motioning him to the surface. He smiled, pushed gently off the bottom, and let his face break the surface of the pool. Only then did he let out the breath he'd been holding.

It hadn't even been hard.

"How did I do?" Garik moved his arms back and forth, treading water.

"Don't start. You know you broke every record set on every leaderboard here."

"I know." Garik swam to the side, and he pulled himself up on his elbows, with his forearms overlapping on the coping. "I just wanted to hear you say it."

"Now's the real test. You're going up against Justin

Kurtew. Are you sure you want to do this?" Christian was a kind soul, the reason the military didn't appreciate his skills. His DNA recombined with that of a wolfhound had been eminently successful at one thing, however, precognition. The only way to harvest that was to harvest the man. Only pulling him in to train Garik was postponing the inevitable, that was, unless Jantzen Hefferly, the number two man in charge of the human-hybrid program, could effect his escape.

They hadn't yet figured out how to work that out.

"I don't have a choice, Christian." Garik dropped back into the water, then with his hands on the side, he vaulted forward, surging out of the water and bringing about a quarter of the pool with him. "You've seen the outcome, though. Right?"

Precog. Christian had a twelve-hour window of events that centered directly around him. The military overlords had hoped for more, and that's why Garik's DNA was intermingled with that of a timber wolf. He was to be the success to Christian's failure.

"Not without injury."

"Grr. That's not the future I wanted you to imagine for me." Garik's precog ability was zilch. Nada. No such thing. Today, Colonel Brace and Senior Airman Vang had scheduled a second round of tests for Garik, to see if he had improved from his first. Garik had failed that one miserably. This one had to be successful. Otherwise, both he and Christian were likely to be written off.

"I've explained," Christian said, as he handed Garik a towel. "I don't imagine the futures I see. They are just there."

"I know." Garik toweled his hair. Another four weeks had given him at least enough to hide his scalp. He still couldn't believe they had *cut it off* when they inducted him—*kidnapped him*—into the human-hybrid project. Of all the things they had done to him, that had been the cruelest.

At times, he wished his girlfriend, Marisa, had never hit that button on the elevator that took them down into the bowels of the Corona Tower basements. He could be enjoying his senior year at Bay City High, instead of swimming laps in this pool and preparing to fight a killer with extra joints in his arms and the ability to sling knives faster than the eye could see.

He could only pray he would survive.

Well, that and trust Christian's precog. He didn't look forward to his injuries. He did notice one thing Christian hadn't shared with him.

What damage would Justin inflict? Garik hadn't asked, because if he knew, he might not show up for the fight at all.

"MOVE INTO the ring, if you will."

Garik took a deep breath and caught Justin's aroma. Anger flowed from the oddly jointed man in brown soil and green plants, dead leaves and growing things. Justin Kurtew scowled at him, for once not wearing the leather duster that seemed to be his standard item of clothing. Garik glanced around the gaming center to see who had spoken. Sitting in a row of chairs, a posse of evaluators, including Weston Rodheimer, Colonel Brace, Airman Vang, and Dr. Jimenez, was poised to critique the competition, to judge whether Garik could continue in the program or be thumped aside like a noisome insect that had buzzed the inside of the screen far too long.

"Now, please." This time, the "please" punched the air a little harder, its impatience showing its face.

Garik realized they were talking to him, seventeen-year-old Garik Shayk, who should be a senior at Bay City High and living with his aunt Irina and her boyfriend, Arik Oblonsky, not here preparing to battle a deadly opponent. He should be getting ready for a skateboard competition, doing his homework, or spending the evening with his girlfriend, Marisa, not trying to save the life of a friend by fighting a deadly assassin.

Garik's first visit to the gaming center surged into his thoughts, reminding him how deadly today might be. Justin Kurtew had been in the ring against Alyna Lindberg, who was modified with a Komodo dragon, giving her retractable claws that were more steel knives than bony keratin. Justin had bested her, and she had walked away with minimal injuries only because

Jantzen Hefferly had restrained him, forcing him to call the battle a draw.

Today, only Garik and Justin were present, both in boxing robes, although this was less boxing than bare knuckle fighting. Well, on Justin's side, bare *knife* fighting. It was Garik who was restricted to his knuckles.

Justin had come alone. Garik was accompanied by Christian. Justin's motivation today was validation. He wanted to prove his position in the hierarchy of the project—and perhaps eat Garik if he bested him. That was the mantis in him. Justin had already been thumped aside as a hybrid failure. He had nothing to lose. Garik was the one with his future on the line. His and Christian's, making his showing in the upcoming foray a vital link to his continued existence.

The two contestants dropped their robes, revealing very different fighting stances. Justin, mated with the DNA of a praying mantis, had a long, almost segmented body, and his forearms had extra joints, allowing him phenomenal fighting speed. Garik's was the tight body of a honed seventeen-year-old. His four weeks under Christian's tutelage had changed him from casual skateboarder to hardened athlete.

Garik's trump card would be the endurance that was a byproduct of his DNA infusion, timber wolf, which Christian had assured him would turn the tide in this battle against his very formidable foe.

At the starting signal, Garik didn't even see Justin's hands move when he felt something bite into his right arm. A gash opened in his skin from the wrist nearly to his elbow, and a volcano of blood welled up, spewing anger like molten rock. Garik stood frozen in shock for a moment, chanting to himself, "Anger gets me nothing. I must use my hands, my mind, my desire to achieve." Then Justin drew his arms back for another strike, sank the tip of a blade in Garik's shoulder, and Garik said, "Forget using my mind." He whipped around and smashed a foot into Justin's ribcage. As his opponent doubled over, he leaped on his back, repeating what he'd watched Jantzen Hefferly do. Justin seemed frozen in a rainbow haze as Garik wrapped his arms under Justin's and pulled them upward, holding the man tight, letting his opponent's arms beat the air, his knives useless against someone he couldn't reach.

There was no bell. No one called time. The rainbows faded as the observers let the moment go on, and on, and on, until Justin, quivering with exhaustion, dropped his knives and bled the words, "I give."

Garik was drained and his muscles burned. He dropped Justin and offered him a hand to stand. Justin glared, but he took Garik's hand before limping away, rubbing his shoulders.

Garik's arm and shoulder? Pound for pound, blood for blood, the price was one he was glad to pay.

— 2 —

olonel Brace, with the solid, white-haired grace of a Southern gentleman, stood and took a firm step toward Dr. Jimenez. He took his hand and pulled him in close and whispered, "Any evidence of the precognition we saw in the other one?"

Garik felt his knees cut from under him. Didn't they see *anything?* He had taken down Justin, one of the deadliest hybridized humans in the complex, well, except for Laura, with her hydrogen cyanide breath, but he'd never seen her actually use it, so he supposed that it didn't count, yet.

He also had never faced her in combat, and he crossed his fingers he never would.

Still—

Christian took his injured arm, lifted it, and pressed a damp cloth against it. Garik turned to him, "Can you believe that man?"

"Justin? It's what I predicted—"

"No." Garik pulled his arm away and pointed to the men across the room who had come to evaluate his progress. "That one."

Colonel Brace had his back to them in an intense discussion with Weston Rodheimer, the director and head researcher at the Corona Tower research complex. Neither man seemed to be aware of Garik's fury.

"Your arm, please." Christian grasped his wrist, worked the cloth over the red area, and pulled it back, perplexed. "I do have the correct arm, yes?"

"Of course, you do. I'm sorry I pulled it away. I get angry, and I don't think. Thank you for helping me." Garik was sorry if he had offended Christian, but still, how inconsiderate and pig-headed could a person be?

"Your other arm, please." Christian held out one of his pawlike hands, waiting patiently.

"He didn't hurt it. It was my shoulder—" Garik looked down, reached his hand to where he'd felt the knife, and pulled it away. There was blood, but he couldn't find the wound. He looked at his other shoulder, and that was when he caught his arm. The red whelps from his fight with a mirror had long since faded, but he had distinctly felt the blade of Justin's knife slice through his skin. He rubbed the skin with his thumb, and he could just see a white line, like that of an old scar, that quickly faded away.

Garik looked at Christian, then at the men across the room. He remembered Jantzen's caution: *Don't give away everything you can do.* This was something new, and they didn't know. He didn't think they needed to, either.

"Wrap it, Christian." Garik turned to hide the arm from the other side of the room.

"No need. Let me clean away—"

"No. Now, Christian. Wrap it. You saw the wound. They did, too. Now, wrap it."

"Okay . . . *oh, I see.*" The big man pulled out a large swath of bandaging, and he began to bind Garik's arm, covering everywhere the skin had been sliced.

"Hurry. My shoulder, too. Here they come." Garik glanced at the colonel, still in earnest discussion with Rodheimer, but definitely headed his direction.

"Here." Christian cut a thick square of padding, added tape, and handed it to Garik. "Put that on your shoulder."

"It's too clean. It won't look real." Garik handed it back.

"How am I supposed to fix that?"

Garik didn't know. "Bloody it up, and fast!" He

could hear the men talking, and they were discussing how fast they could expect Garik's injuries to heal.

"Why me?" Christian's shoulders dropped, and it seemed his whole body deflated like an old balloon. He took the scissors, jabbed it into his palm, and pressed it to the outside of the bandage. After a moment, he smeared it around and handed it back to Garik.

"Perfect. Thanks." Garik pressed it to his shoulder just as Weston Rodheimer began to speak.

"I've seen Justin in bloodlust before." Rodheimer glanced to the shoulder, nodding at the blood, and he dropped his eyes to Garik's arm. Garik held it against his chest, covering it with his other hand and trying to disguise the lack of blood. "Only one man's been able to stop him before. Impressive, no, Dr. Jamie?"

"But the other matter we discussed—" Brace dismissed Christian, his disappointment clear, and he shifted his eyes to Garik. "We must begin to see evidence of—"

"Enough for now, Colonel." Rodheimer held out a massive hand, with a palm almost apelike in its girth. "He anticipated an attack and thwarted it, even if he didn't realize what he was doing. I'd say that's proof enough, at least for now."

"Yes, Director, but I expect more."

"And I'm certain you will get it. Now, follow me," and Rodheimer turned his attention from Garik, walking away as he broached a new subject.

"Your robe, my liege." Christian stood, and he bowed slightly, offering the boxing robe opened and ready for Garik's arms. He had his injured hand wrapped with a large strip of bandaging tape.

"I know what a liege is, and I'm not your superior—or your boss." Garik backed into the robe anyway, trusting it to hide his pretend damage. He pushed his left, unbandaged arm through, and he let Christian drape the robe over his right shoulder, leaving the sleeve hanging loose. Christian tied the sash, leaving just Garik's hand exposed.

As they exited the gaming center, Garik thought about Joanie. Her DNA was mated with a jellyfish to enable longevity. Even eternal life. They had no real way to test it, other than killing her, and they hadn't chosen to do that, thank the afterlife gods that be.

He cringed to think how they might try to test his new skill, and every way he imagined was worse than the death it might bring.

GARIK SAT atop the examining table with his shirt off and swung his feet back and forth, a double pendulum, each foot providing a counterbalance for the other. He pushed harder, bored, wishing he could get back to the part of the complex where he belonged.

The door opened.

"Mr., um, Garik, my boy." Dr. Jimenez painted a wide smile on his face. "At least your legs work. How's that arm and that shoulder?"

"Fine, Dr. Jamie." He smiled and slowed his legs. He didn't need Jimenez to be too concerned or too inquisitive. "Christian rewrapped it just before I came down. He says it's healing perfectly."

"Okay. I don't see any seepage, so that's good. I didn't see the cut on your arm when it happened, but I saw the one on your shoulder. I should look at that one. If the muscle was torn—"

"I don't feel anything." Garik lifted his arm and rotated his shoulder in its socket. He definitely didn't need the doctor removing the bandage to find no damage underneath at all. "Christian is great at this stuff. He's taking good care of me. Thank you, Dr. Jamie, for letting him train me. My success is your success. Without you, I probably wouldn't be here any longer." He smiled brightly. Convincingly, he hoped.

"At least let me check your range of motion." Dr. Jimenez took Garik's left wrist in one hand, his upper arm in the other, and forced the limb as hard and far as he dared. "That doesn't hurt?"

"Not at all, Dr. Jamie. Do you want to try the other arm, too?" Garik tried to keep anticipation on his face, a hopeful look that the doctor might find something wrong that needed fixed.

"No, that's fine." Jimenez stepped back, pulled a tablet and stylus from a pocket, and marked several things. He glanced at Garik, motioned with the stylus, and said, "You may go. Tell Christian he has my approval."

"Thank you, Dr. Jamie. I sure will." Garik hopped down, grabbed his shirt from the back of a chair, and began slipping it on as he backed out of the room. "Next week?"

The doctor glanced at him, Garik already forgotten. "Sure, sure. Check with Leah."

"Right-o, Dr. Jamie." Garik turned, let the door close behind him, and rubbed his left shoulder. The man was a monster. He had twisted his shoulder just to make it hurt.

Still, this was about Christian, and for that, there was *almost* no pain that Garik wouldn't endure.

Now, however, Devon was waiting at the climbing wall. The man didn't care about the bandage on his arm. He just wanted to climb.

Well, that was perfect to Garik, because that's exactly what he wanted, too.

JOHN CARTER and Paolo Leveen showed up at the climbing wall while Garik and Devon Maye, the recreation and activities director, were in harnesses overhead.

John, blond and fitter, if possible, than Devon, was wearing a climbing harness, and he called, "Devon, hey! Can anyone use this wall?"

"Anyone who's good enough." Devon was alongside Garik. Garik was in a harness with a safety line attached. Devon held a remote control to the safety line's overhead winch.

Garik, despite his bandaged arm and shoulder, hadn't needed it even one time.

"That's me, then." John dropped an equipment bag from over his shoulder, letting it fall heavily to the floor. Far overhead, in the three windows that broached the next level up, giving a view to the military personnel housed on Level 1, several bored Airmen leaned on handrails that ran the length of the windows. One pointed, John waved, and the Airman waved back.

"Friends, John?"

"With everyone." John called for Paolo to grab a safety, that he was going up first.

Devon held out his remote, adjusted the winch to take up some of Garik's slack, and moved to a new purchase on the wall. He called for the young man to try a new grip, perhaps one of the orange.

"Orange?" Garik called. "You trust me, now?"

"I trust the safety line." Devon held out his hand, touched the remote, and the winch whined, pulling the safety line tight until Garik's harness bit into his backside.

"Okay, okay. I'm going." Garik reached for an orange, and when he moved, the pressure on his harness eased.

"You'll make it, kiddo. You've got this."

"Right-o, Devon-o." Garik grinned and gave him a thumbs up. That was a mistake, as his left hand began to slip, and only the safety line was there to break his fall.

"I told you," Devon scolded him. "No fancy moves with that injured shoulder. Now, hold on while I move you back to the wall."

The winch began to whine, and when he was close enough, Garik reached for a blue grip, only to have Devon call, "No, not the blue. I told you, that's for when you get good."

Garik grinned and reached for orange.

GARIK STOOD under the shower head in the changing rooms located near the climbing wall. He was glad to have his bandages off, and they sat on the seat just outside the shower beside his limited-access passkey.

John and Paolo were in their own showers, the reason they had "happened" to show up at the climbing wall at the same time as Devon and Garik. No one could be allowed to hear their plans to break Christian out of the research facility, and this was the only place they could be together without raising suspicion.

John was already out when Garik emerged into the common area around the sinks. He carried his bandages, wanting to wait as long as possible before reattaching them.

"A real fall?" John adjusted his belt with a grin,

looking up just long enough to wink.

"It kept Devon's attention, didn't it?" Garik slipped his shirt on and kicked his towel near the used towel bin. He sat on a bench to put on his shoes.

They both looked up to see Paolo watching them, already in the room without them noticing.

"You, there, and you, Garik. So, what are our plans to get Christian out? It's been a month. We're running out of time."

Garik looked from Paolo to John and back to Paolo. He was still in training, and Christian was his trainer. They had plenty of time to plan a way out for Christian, didn't they?

Or was there something he didn't know?

— 3 —

B

efore they could work out a rescue plan for Christian, Garik was summoned to the research center's main office block on Level 1. Van Hermoso accompanied him, not quite a guard, but never letting Garik out of his sight. The office block was tucked out of the way behind the main elevator shaft connecting the under-ground complex of dungeon-like spaces directly to the mall, the lobby, and the upper floors of Corona Tower—and off-limits to program participants of the hybridized sort.

So, the reason behind Garik's visit? He knew it

must be big—meaning bad for him—if they wanted him here. He had only visited once, and that was with Jantzen Hefferly, the number two man on campus. Van pulled out his passkey when they reached the office block, inserted it by a door, and it required his hand, also. He pressed it to the panel, a red light scanned the vein patterns under his skin, and the panel turned green, saying, "Accepted, Van Hermoso. Please retrieve your passkey and enter within thirty seconds."

Garik hesitated to follow.

Van jerked his head to suggest they continue moving, asking, "What is it? Shoot, I'm listening."

"What have I done wrong?" There was no sense in asking *if* he had done anything wrong. There was always another rule to break, one they hadn't shared with him yet.

"Maybe nothing." Van chuckled, not in a mean way, but not being friendly, either. "Then, maybe something. They don't tell me everything, and I don't want them to."

"So, you're glad I'm me and you're you."

"I didn't say that." Van stopped before one door out of many. "We're here. I'm told I won't be escorting you back, but I will see you later. I am your occupational therapist. You are still working on an occupation, I trust."

"Sure, Van, just waiting to see what I can do." He tried to be pleasant, but the sign on the door had dropped a rock in his stomach. IT Oversight and Security Specialist. Computers, information, Internet searches, remote cameras, and . . . listening in to secret conversations, like those that involved getting Christian out of Corona Tower while still alive.

Why had he ever thought the changing rooms were any different than any other thing about this place? Everything was suspect. Everyone and everything. Van likely wouldn't see him later, unless he decided to visit Level 5 and search the cages of mewling and pathetic creatures that were no longer of any use in the human-hybrid project's DNA-enhancement program.

"If you need me, I'm here for you."

"I appreciate that, Van. Maybe I should go in." And get this over with. He imagined how it might go: *What? You thought we were helping Christian escape? No sirs, I am a good wolf, er, boy, and the worst thing I do when you guys aren't watching over my shoulder is howl at the moon. Am I making fun of you? No sirs, I would never do that* . . . sheesh, it was as bad as lying to Dr. Jimenez and watching the man eat up every word.

"That's a good attitude." Van opened the door, and when Garik stepped through, he moved back and let the door close.

The room was disorganized, the space of someone who couldn't focus enough to finish one thing before moving on to another. From a side door, a man, as thin as the tie he wore, stepped inside, bumped an open filing cabinet drawer, and barely kept from spilling the coffee in his hands.

"Oh, hot," he said, touching a dripping finger to his mouth to suck off the excess. "Sorry. Welcome, Mr. Shayk. Come in, come in. Our first time to meet, yes, our very first."

"Okay," Garik said, confused. The man didn't sound like he was being accused of espionage and collusion to aid and abet the escape of one of the Tower's hybridized subjects. Three large computer screens hung from the wall, each one with multiple views, eyes overseeing everything that happened in the room and likely anywhere else the man wanted to look. "So, why am I here?"

"We will get to that. Let me introduce myself. Jeffrey Howard. You may have noticed the sign on the door." Jeffrey looked for a place to set his coffee, moved a book to make room, and offered Garik his hand.

Garik sighed. *If I must.* All the hand shaking. They had *kidnapped* him, but he took the hand. He squeezed harder than he should, causing Jeffrey to massage his hand afterward. *For you, Marisa*, Garik thought, her absence a hollow space in his chest.

"Do you know Andrew?" Jeffrey asked, lifting a pair of glasses from the disarray on his desk.

"Should I?"

"No, no, I don't suppose so. I just thought I would

ask. Oh, his last name is Miner. Any bells, now?" Howard lifted his eyebrows hopefully.

"Still nothing." Garik shrugged. Uncertainty and frustration were eating at his patience and manners. Another minute, and he would have no polite responses left. "You sent for me. Is there something I should know?"

"Oh, yes, yes, yes. A seat, yes—" The man looked around and realized there was nowhere for Garik to sit. "—how about we use the conference room? Andrew will be arriving shortly, yes, shortly. Do you mind waiting?"

He didn't see that he had a choice.

ANDREW MINER was a barrel of a man coming down the corridor. Jeffrey and Garik turned a corner, startling him, and a box in his hand nearly went to the floor. A stack of papers did.

"Safe!" Andrew held the box up, and it seemed Jeffrey breathed a sigh of relief as he scrambled to gather up the papers. Inside the conference room, the box went on the table as though in a place of honor. Andrew introduced himself. "Andrew Miner, Financial Analyst and Fund Coordinator. You give me your funds and I coordinate them." He smiled broadly as though he enjoyed the tagline.

"I don't have any funds, sorry," Garik said, now convinced they were having a stupid contest.

Andrew smiled, "That's a good one," and he announced, "You, young man, are receiving an upgrade."

Garik looked from man to man. Upgrade, like, from wolf boy to werewolf boy? Level up! Open the box to receive your reward. Upgrade your brain and receive amazing gifts. Infinite lives. Super strength . . . none of this made sense.

"You did tell him, Jeffrey?" Andrew looked at skinny Jeffrey.

"I, um, did I tell you, Mr. Shayk?"

"Garik." He closed his eyes to focus and keep his anger under control before looking up, thinking, my mind, my way, anger does no good. "My father is Mr. Shayk. And no, you haven't told me anything."

"Yes, I seem to remember, using your given name was in my notes. So sorry. The Director wishes you to have an upgraded passkey."

Garik's world shifted, and he couldn't keep a smile from his face. He was one step closer to Houdini time, seeing Marisa, telling her about her sister, Marina, that he'd found her; and visiting the skate park with Muhammad, Ibn, and Hayat; giving his aunt a hug; and maybe even going up to see Mrs. Waggoner to find out how her plants were doing—

"Your new apartment will have—"

"What? I'm moving, too?" He tried to think how that would affect his escape plans, its distance to the main elevator . . . any changes could be vital to his plans.

"One thing before we let you go. I have," Andrew stood and rummaged through the box, "your new computer and something else you might enjoy." He lifted out a gaming console. "For your very own."

Jeffrey said, almost hesitatingly, "I have written, um, am writing, you see, because it is in beta phase, a new, um—"

"Stop, Jeffrey." Andrew leaned in to Garik. "Will you test Jeffrey's new video game? You are, well, more—" and he whispered, "—more *normal* than many of our residents. He would appreciate your *normal* opinion."

And give me a reason to gather with my friends. Garik smiled. "Certainly."

Andrew grinned, nodding his success at Jeffrey. He attempted to button his jacket, but it refused to meet around his waist.

GARIK CARRIED the box with the gaming console. Grunt labor, although he didn't mind being the pack mule today. Now, Christian had a reason to be in Garik's apartment, and no one would be looking for something devious or underhanded in their time together outside the recreation area or training cells.

The elevator doors opened. Straight and right would take them to his old room. They made an immediate left, past the emergency clinic with its darkened windows, away from the break area with its fully stocked kitchen, and the opposite direction from the recreation area. People began to fill the corridors, a few at first, then more. Garik recognized many of the faces, even if he didn't know all the names. Christian had been so busy with his training, there hadn't been time for social introductions. At the new apartment, Joseph Howard and Tyrone Brown were just inside the door.

Tyrone flashed his familiar smile, but it was Joseph who spoke. "Weren't sure where you wanted it, and Ty thought near the door. That okay by you?"

"My ZBoard? I didn't expect that. Thanks!" They had already moved the ZBoard's charging unit for him without him having to ask. Rodheimer must have been really impressed with what he saw during his fight with Justin.

"I 'spected you would want it, so when we moved your things, we brought it along."

Garik's eyes went damp. The people at the top could learn something from the little guys on their team. Be nice to the people under you, and they'll be nice to you. How did Kevin Lee used to say it? Leave it like you found it, cleaner if you can.

Garik gave them a nod and said, "You ever need anything, I'll help if I can."

"Thank you. Have a good day." Joseph nodded and touched his temple as if tipping a hat. Tyrone grinned, and Garik nodded back.

Garik still wanted out, would Houdini at the first window, but until then, this was a pretty slick place to be. He couldn't wait until Christian came for a visit.

GARIK TOOK time to explore once everyone left. The apartment had two real rooms. The kitchen was a tiny unit tucked in a nook, but the place had everything he needed, especially a separate bedroom. A living room held a couch and a chair, even a coffee table with two remote controls. He set the box on the coffee table and pulled out the gaming unit.

"So, they love you more."

Garik looked up. Justin stood just inside the door. "Justin," he said, unsure why he was here. He pictured the man's ferocity in the ring, and his stomach turned over, freezing his heart for several beats. He tried to process his best options for the attack he was sure was coming.

"I got demoted." Justin walked in, his attitude casual, almost as if they had something common between them, something besides being hybrid. He looked inside the bedroom and turned back to Garik, his face hardening. He was a gunslinger, ready to draw and fire.

"I didn't ask for this." Garik wanted that between them.

"Yes, you did. When you humiliated me in front of the Director."

"Why are you here, Justin?" Garik would fight, but he didn't want it to come to that.

"I've seen you and your friends together."

"So?" Garik tried to follow the man's intimations, to place what he might be talking about. There was nothing to connect them to anything—

"There." Justin slipped a mini flash drive from his pocket and dropped it on the coffee table. "There's more than one way to listen in on a conversation."

Then he was out the door.

— 4 —

R

acquetball. Who would have thought being in a white, windowless room *by yourself* and whacking a tiny ball could be so satisfying?

Garik tossed the ball up, swung his racquet, felt the impact of the racquet against the ball feed down his forearm, followed by the rewarding *whack* of the rubber sphere against the far wall. The sound in the contained, hard space reverberated in his ears.

He leaped, caught the ball on the return, and *whack*.

Over and over as sweat ran down his face, and his shirt and shorts clung to him like wet rags.

Whack! For Marisa. I'm not in Russia, Mari.

Whack! Hayat, skateboarding together off curbs.

Garik's eyes blurred. He pressed his face to his shoulders, a quick move in between leaping for the ball, unable to admit to the emotions.

Whack! Ibn, I miss you, my friend.

Whack! Robbie, my little brother.

Whack! I need a hug, Iri.

Whack! Muhammad, Allah be praised.

Garik grinned when he thought of Muhammad, even as his heart burned.

Whack! Wesji. *Whack!* Wajeha. *Whack!* Vladimir and Giorgio. *Whack!* Mrs. Waggoner. *Whack!* The three shrimps. And Alexi. Regina. Everyone, *whack, whack, whack!*

Whack! For Garik, who's lost and can't find his way back again.

Garik half squatted, his elbows resting on his knees, his emotions ripping air from his throat, and his need to breathe shoving it back in. The blue rubber ball came to rest at his feet, and he watched it roll to a stop.

Justin. *Justin!* Anger tore through him.

Garik had played the mini flash drive. His voice, Paolo's and John's had all been there. There was no mistaking the complicity among the three.

Justin! Of all people!

Garik adjusted the legs of his shorts, unsticking the fabric from his skin, and giving himself room to flex and move. He leaned toward the ball and grasped it in his hand, compressing the hollow sphere, flattening it before tossing it into the air.

A thing few people could easily do.

Whack! Garik watched as the ball passed the service line, slammed into the front wall, returned to him and impacted him right between the eyes. His legs gave out under him, knocking him hard on the short line. His racquet skittered across the floor.

Clapping echoed into the hard-walled space, and Garik looked behind him. Through the glass back wall, Joanie McDonald raised an arm, yelled, "Hoot, hoot!" and slammed a palm against the glass. Sandwiched between her hand and the glass was a package of mints. "Mint, barker boy?"

"Not my name," he called, his face heating with shame. "And no."

"Your way." She yanked open the door and shrugged in the same motion, and she paused before entering. "Your permission?"

"Yeah, Joanie. Come in."

Garik drew his knees up, wrapped his arms around them, and watched the ball. It was still rolling, and it hit the wall, skittered off, and came to a stop.

"Angry game." She dropped beside him, her legs crossed.

"Angry game," he confirmed. He lifted his shirt, pressed it to his face, and dropped it. "Do you need something?"

She reached into her pocket and opened her hand to reveal a mini flash drive.

"Justin." Garik's shoulders sagged. He'd thought he was already as miserable as he could be, but he realized there were always more depths to plumb. The man would be their undoing.

"Ideas?" Joanie popped two of the mints in her mouth and crunched one.

"You play?" He motioned around the court.

"Yeah. Not this. You stink." She pointed a finger at him and grinned. "Shower." She thumbed toward the door and stood.

Garik unraveled himself and joined her, gathering the ball and the racquet on the way. Who else had received a flash drive? He could kick himself. No place was private, no matter what they said. Any word anywhere could be recorded.

He'd do well to remember that.

GARIK ENTERED the changing rooms for the recreation area, the one where he had injured his hand on the broken mirror. A posse of runners, likely off-duty researchers, were pulling on sleeveless jerseys and joking with one another and laughing. One man was seated and tying the laces on a pair of purple and white running shoes. He pushed his tall socks to his ankles before standing and tossed a towel over one shoulder.

Street clothes hung on hooks and spilled out of bags, with some scattered on the floor.

The men's glances told Garik that he was different, unwelcome, although they didn't say it. He made his way through them to the showers, grabbed a towel and soap on the way, and tried to block out the sounds of friends enjoying one another's company.

By the time he was out, they were gone, although their things were not. He looked around, certain Justin's recording device was likely still in place. He had maybe an hour before they returned. He began running his fingers under the edges of the benches, moving the men's shoes and clothing, and occasionally scrunching his nose at an item with an especially strong odor.

He was on the third bench when he heard the familiar, "Hey, kiddo, there you are."

"Yeah, Devon." He trusted the activities director, and he continued to search.

"Looking for you. I saw Joanie in the break area, and she pointed me here."

"You found me." He returned two satchels under the bench and stood to move toward the next one.

"You're okay? I mean, you and Christian. He's doing you right?" Devon glanced around the room, taking in the disarray. "Have you taken on some sort of cleanup duty?"

"Yeah, cleanup duty. Devon, I don't have time to chat. Anything specific?" Garik heard Joanie coming out in him. Then, patience wasn't his thing at the moment.

"It's the next mall event. A new group, the Ace Holes." He chuckled and winked. "Really, Ace of Holes, but—" He shrugged like it was a really good joke.

"Okay." Garik dropped and leaned under the bench. He didn't care much about the Ace of Holes. He needed Justin's recording device.

"So, do you want to go?"

"Go?" Garik pulled out from under the bench and looked at him. "To an event?"

"Yes." Devon pushed a bag out of the way and sat on a bench.

"I don't have permission. Last time, I was there only because Jantzen had me on a leash. Sorry, Devon." He dropped back under the bench and satisfied himself that it was recording device free before reemerging.

"What *are* you looking for?"

"Not stinky socks." Garik wrinkled his nose. "Every one of these guys has his own stinky smell, and I'm going to choke."

"About the event." Devon leaned forward, his elbows on his knees. He grinned. "Jantzen's already said you can go."

"Why?" Garik could hardly focus on Devon's invitation. He had a recording device on his mind, and he didn't know how long he had until the running posse returned. He knelt and began to feel under the sinks.

"Party, kiddo. I need to teach you how. Hey, whatever, let me help you look." Devon crossed the room, chose the next sink, knelt to see what was underneath.

"Okay, Devon, I'm looking for a microphone or something that can record a conversation."

"Oh, easy. Done." Devon stood and slammed the cabinet door.

"You have it?" Garik sat with his knees on the floor, surprised the man found it so quickly.

"Not with me. It's in my office."

Not Devon! Garik could hardly believe the rec director was complicit with Justin in recording private conversations in the changing rooms. He felt his trust in the man bleeding away.

"Are you with Justin, then?" Of course, he was.

"Justin, you mean, Kurtew? I don't get the connection."

"But you have the microphone."

"I sa—*id* that." Devon rocked his head to the side, drawing out the word. "You, my friend, need a distraction, like a party." He grinned. "On the mall!"

"Okay, I'll go, but first, tell me how you have the microphone I'm looking for." Sheesh! Yes, this was proof. Every single person in this place was a total and complete idiot, perhaps even him!

"What you people don't clean, I have to police. This

mess?" He motioned around the room. "I can report the people here if I know who leaves it, but if they don't clean it, it's up to me. So, Garik, my friend, clean up after yourself!" He laughed.

"Leave it like you found it, cleaner if you can." Kevin Lee's philosophy. In the moment, Garik missed the martial arts teacher, even if he had barely known him. He was from outside, his life before this place, from Bay City, from a connection that had been broken and was now more desirable than ever.

"Perfect! You, kiddo, understand perfectly. So, we're on? Friday?" Devon with his blond cowlick grinned expectantly.

"Right-o, Devon." Garik lifted a hand, calling, "Bam, done."

"Ha, ha!" Devon laughed and disappeared out the door.

Garik took in a deep breath. Devon. Trees and water. He was surprised he could find the man in all the surrounding stink, and it did stink, all nine of the researchers, each one as individual as the parts of a machine.

Then he realized he'd been able to smell Devon through the rank stable of odors all along. If he met these men again, he'd know each of them by their smell. And it wasn't something he would likely ever forget.

GARIK ARRIVED on the mall.

He hadn't expected his passkey to work one of the main elevators, but finding out it did wouldn't help him out of the basement research complex. At least he understood how the hybrids like him could join the events on the mall without chaperones. Once the wall went up, enclosing the mall, the elevators accepted the passkeys given to the research subjects.

Be home by midnight, Cinderella. Or no pumpkins for you!

More likely, they would turn into pumpkins if they weren't underground when the walls were banished back into the sidewalks by their fairy godmothers.

No lost glass shoes for you! Back, back underground where you live!

Garik could run his fingers through his hair, now. It was enough to show some curl, although not to tie back into a bun. The thought of Marisa, her hands at his neck that day they visited the Tower with Kevin Lee. And now, here he was, living in the Tower.

Well, the *basements,* like a *thing,* a deformed uncle you were afraid to show to the world.

The wind whipped past him when he stepped outside, thrusting chilled fingers down his jacket. He touched the flash drive he carried in his pocket, afraid to leave it anywhere. Devon had invited Annie Vanschooneveld to join them. Annie had dark eyes, and her red lipstick accentuated her big teeth when she smiled. Her hair was pulled back, and her face was softened by long bangs that covered her eyebrows.

Annie was the reason for Garik's jacket.

"Garik, Annie." They had shown up at Garik's door dressed warmly. "Annie's the foreign affairs attaché."

"Hello, Garik." She held out a slender hand to shake.

"Foreign, like other countries?"

"Yes, I'm away more than I'm here. This is my first time to get to attend an event. Devon insisted I come. You've been before?" She smiled.

"Once." He shook her hand, noticing how Devon looked at her when she was talking. He wondered if that was how he'd watched Marisa, and in the image in his head, he also recalled her words to him to *pay attention.*

The memory made him smile.

"You enjoyed it, then." She turned to Devon. "You said it didn't go well."

Devon shrugged and looked down, his Nordic skin flaming with streaks of red under his cheekbones. Annie asked Garik if he was planning on a coat. Garik looked at Devon for clarification, and Devon agreed he should.

Yea, Annie!

Outside, the night wasn't yet fully dark, and around him, Bay City stretched south, rising in elevation toward Stanwick Hill. In the distance, he could just see the Ransom Communications Building with its rack of antennae thrust skyward and illuminated. To its right was his home, except for the other buildings in the way.

Home. Marisa. His friends. He blinked his eyes to clear them and put on a smile. He was at a party, and it was his night to have a good time.

The Ace of Holes was here! Yea!

He stepped into the food court and past the tables he and his friends used to gather around. Out from under the building, the wall surrounding the mall blocked the view of anything at eye level.

He was at the ball. He had gotten his wish, and it wasn't what he thought it would be.

— 5 —

T

he Ace of Holes logo spilled across the marquee on the mall's large sign. The image of a card wearing a giant ace of spades twirled, and a gun sent a bullet flying through the center, punching clean through the black ace and stopping the card's spin. The words "Ace of Holes" spilled out, accompanied by streamers and fireworks until they filled up the massive screen.

"Have fun, you two! I'm going to search for my friends." Garik waved to Devon and Annie, certain they wanted to be alone.

"Have fun!" Annie waved, and she tucked her arm

in Devon's, the way Garik wished Marisa had tucked hers in his. They had forgotten him before he turned away.

As he searched the crowd, it crossed his mind that if Annie were allowed to attend, so could people like Jeffrey Howard and Andrew Miner. He tried to picture the thin man with his glasses, together with the balding barrel of a man. He couldn't do it.

He did find Airman Wu Han. As with last time, military types were scattered across the mall, likely to ensure that the hybrids attending the event kept their sometimes burgeoning and rampant killer instincts under control. Thank you, Justin, for teaching me that, Garik thought sourly. He headed Wu's direction, hoping to renew a connection with someone he had enjoyed and looked up to.

He was waylaid by Airman Vang.

"Ah, Mr. Shayk. I see you are once more with us for one of our shows."

"Yes. I'm sorry, Mr. Vang. I'm hoping to catch someone. Do you mind?" Garik tried to keep Wu in sight, but he couldn't maintain a conversation with the short Vang and look out across the mall at the same time.

"I will not keep you long. I wish to congratulate you on your performance against Mr. Kurtew. I understand the Director has upgraded your accommodations. Well earned. Enjoy your evening, Mr. Shayk."

"Thank you, Airman." Garik stepped away, now unable to find Airman Han. He took a deep breath and quieted his emotions. Even when he was being nice, Airman Vang was a wrecking ball battering the best things about Garik's day.

"Garik!"

A hand clapped him on the shoulder. Garik turned to a familiar face.

"Jantzen, hi. I haven't seen Christian today."

"No." He didn't offer an explanation. "Perhaps he can make it tonight. I see you're back on good terms with the Airman."

"Speaking, anyway. He speaks, and I don't." Garik heard the criticism, and he knew Jantzen understood. A month ago, he'd have not dared say that. Maybe in anger, but then he'd be forced to apologize and accept the consequences.

"Sometimes best. They are our overlords. He who controls the purse strings, and that they do."

"Feel for me. I'm the peon." That's the way he felt, too. On the raised area where the Ace of Holes would perform, the action was getting under way. The Ace of Holes was a magic venue, and they had a live elephant on the stage with three men attempting to control it. "I need to find my friends."

"Go north. I suggested they meet you there. That's the one spot you'll be able to see some of the Tower's light show."

"It's not real, Jantzen. You made that clear."

"Suit yourself. I must mingle. Maybe we will bump into each other later. If not, lunch tomorrow?"

Garik hesitated. Did the man know about Justin's recording? Is that why he wanted to have lunch with him?

"Or not?" Jantzen glanced around, his eyes already taking in the people he intended to connect with. If there was an ulterior motive, Garik couldn't find it.

"Okay. Sure, why not. I'll see you then."

Jantzen clenched a fist at chest level, shook it and grinned. "Enjoy the show, my friend." He turned, calling to a woman with long, black bangs that did a poor job of covering a scar on her forehead. "Angelica, do you have a minute?"

CHOW DOWN in the actual food court might be shuttered for the night's event, but tonight's magic show was a very different performance than the Howling Pterodactyl's energy-infused assault on people's senses. Numerous Chow Down food kiosks were set up across the mall, with "street-friendly" fare: hot links, burgers, and cheese-covered nachos. Garik was several blocks in when Giselle placed a hand on his arm.

"There you are, Garik. Come. I've been sent to reel you in." She winked at him, smiling.

"You like Paolo. Why do you smile at everyone like that?"

"Oh, poo." She blew out her cheeks. "How do you see through me so easily?" Still, she wrapped one arm in his, and she walked right up against him.

"No one can miss it." Garik felt the pressure of her arm. She wasn't Marisa, so it meant nothing to him.

"Except Paolo."

"I know."

"Oh, you! Why I volunteered to come find you, I'll never know." She pulled her arm away, and she made a pouty face.

He shrugged. "I could have found you guys. I didn't need someone to find me. I always know just where I am. Besides, I would have expected Julia."

"Right. Heat-sensing. Too many people to single you out."

"I didn't think of that."

They walked for a bit together. This far out, the crowds were thinner, and the night sky was growing darker. Behind Corona Tower, the two-story parking garage seemed truncated next to the glass skyscraper. Headlights flashed inside, someone exiting, likely, and he remembered the family that was arriving for a visit at Stamford Suites the day Marisa and he fell down the elevator into the lair that had trapped him. Likely, who-ever was in that vehicle was a Stamford Suites guest, in the tower for a night or two, and out to freedom when-ever they pleased.

At some point, Giselle had encircled her arm around

his again, and when they reached the table where the others were, she patted his arm, looked up at him, and purred, only stopping when it was clear that Paolo was paying no attention.

Alyna was seated next to Paolo, and she was showing him something. Garik couldn't see what.

Joanie called to him, "Gari! Made it! Whoop, Devon! Convinced you!"

"Yah, twisted my arm."

"Glad he did. Fun show, tonight." Joanie's mohawk seemed to be painted brighter than ever, or maybe it was catching the light of the setting sun over the distant water in the harbor. She looked down, pulled out a fresh package of mints, opened them and popped one before looking away.

Leigh and Laura waved. They were deep in a discussion, and Garik didn't pay much mind. John was returning from a food kiosk, bare-armed in the chill, and he walked up behind Garik, bumping his elbow to Garik's shoulder.

"We've been waiting on you." He nodded at the others, several of them intent on something or the other. "Have you heard—"

He was interrupted by Joanie, who called, "Nachos! Here, John. You! The very, very best."

"I'll be right back, Garik. What I've got to discuss is important."

Marco, with his lemur's tail showing more distinct

stripes than when Garik had first met him, sidled up to a table, seeming to appear out of nowhere, and he reached for the food John held.

Joanie was standing by then, and she had John by the elbow, pulling him out of Marco's reach. She tugged him to her table, farther from Garik and the answer to the question in his mind.

Important? What do you mean important? And . . . and . . . you're going to leave me hanging out there?

Sheesh, John! What have I ever done to you?

JULIA CANTOS was the final person Garik noticed.

"Julia, I didn't see you there." He remembered: not moving and not being seen were part of Julia's camouflage.

"I could sense you from a block away." She pointed the direction of the Tower. "Look. The world's seen nothing like it. A miracle. A giant structure of glass and steel, and there it is. Bam, blowing up right before our eyes. THE BUILDING." She said her final two words like capital letters, and she laughed, ending in a rasping cough. "Sorry, I'll need some gum on that note."

Garik followed her arm. Close to the base, the Tower looked normal, as always, but as he raised his eyes, he could see the familiar silicon glitter flash in the sky, as the Tower shattered into a million pieces and fell, flashing in brilliance to the ground, only to lift back into the sky and reform the Tower into a whole once again.

Except that the effect didn't extend all the way to the ground. The angle of the projectors, perhaps, or some other way that the image refracted from this angle; whatever, the shattering tower was incomplete. And, from here, it was just possible to see the dim imprint of the Tower impressed into the black velvet of the night sky even as the glitter showered the street, thereby ruining the effect.

"Not as pretty as when seen from the city." He shrugged, not impressed, and turned away, taking the seat next to Julia and falling into it.

"Got that right. Most things are prettier from the outside. What I see is best of all." She slipped a stick of gum in her mouth, and she chewed it twice before she began to pop it.

"What do you see that's best?" Garik needed a better way to see everything about his situation.

"I see the inside you." She cupped her hands in the air, framing him.

"Ah. Body heat."

"And you have a lot going on in there. I predict you're about to evolve. We all do once we take the drug."

"The modified DNA serum." He wasn't sure he was ready.

"Julia." John slipped in beside them. "Garik, has anyone talked to you?"

"Yah, Julia's said a mouthful." He grinned, and John laughed.

"I imagine. No, about this." He pulled out a flash drive identical to the one Justin had dropped on Garik's coffee table.

"I'm not getting left out of this little party." Julia worked a cord from around her neck. She also had one of the drives.

As did every person in the group.

"JANTZEN ACTED like there might be a problem with Christian earlier." Garik had a rash of pitted prunes in his stomach—the pits not the prunes. "Is it possible that Justin's that big a fool?"

"What benefit could he get from it?" Giselle pushed her lips into a pouty shape, and she wilted into her chair.

"Revenge. He wants to get even with me." Garik knew it could be the only answer. He'd heard the man's words, that he had been *demoted*.

"It's more than just you besting him in the ring." Paolo tapped his claw-like nails on the tabletop. "He's been, maybe not bested, but restrained many times. If he wanted revenge, there's almost everyone on the campus he'd have to take revenge on."

"Does he have a conflict with Christian? Maybe that's the difference."

Leigh cleared her throat. Tonight, she wore a full

sharkskin coat, with a tight collar and large, oversized pockets. When she had their attention, she half stood, then dropped back down. Laura placed her hand on her arm, and Leigh brushed it off and stood.

"Christian has a conflict with nobody, except those fools." She pointed, and sure enough Rodheimer and Sunchaser were coming their way.

Alyna's claws flexed, giving off a rubbing sound each time they slipped in or out.

Marco dropped to the floor of the mall, and his voice hissed from under the table, "Maybe backing out is the thing to do."

Laura leaned under the table and hissed, "No, you little weasel, you."

"I'm not a weasel, you, you, worm, you. I'm a *lemur*."

"And John's a wood frog, and he doesn't hide under the tables. Get up here, you weasel." Laura reached under the table, grabbed the nape of his neck, and forced him to sit in a chair.

Hands throughout the group wrapped around mini flash drives, making them disappear as one.

Weston Rodheimer appeared out of the darkness, occluding the better part of the night, while dragging behind him a dark raincloud of muted shadow. Halo Sunchaser basked in his wake, tall and spare to his immense proportions.

"Joanie," Rodheimer began, recognizing the

accepted leader of the group. He nodded at Garik. "I see you've claimed the boy."

"He needed claiming." Joanie gave a complete sentence, clearly to appease the man.

"See, Halo, she can construct a complete sentence."

"As you say, Weston." Sunchaser nodded, but her eyes were soaking up the boy, like he had something she would like to possess if only given the opportunity.

Garik felt the drive in his hand press into his skin. He prayed to himself, *Not now. They can't know. Please don't let Justin have told.*

"Okay," Rodheimer announced. "The party is there. Break this up and act like you're enjoying it."

The man held his position until the group on the edge of the mall began to shift position and move away.

Garik found himself with Marco, as the others broke off to go different directions. He double-checked his pocket, wishing now he'd left the little memory device anywhere else. That had been so close.

"Are we giving up?" Marco tugged at his sleeve. "Huh, Garik? You've been spending the most time with him. Are we giving up?"

"I'm not." He glared at the little lemur man. He had *jumped* under the *table.* Who does that?

He knew the real question should be *what* does that?

"And good heavens, Marco, what is that smell?"

"I was nervous." Marco's tail flicked back and

forth. "I do that when I get nervous. Sorry."

"Do what, wet yourself?" It was much worse than that.

"I marked your leg." Marco shrugged. "It happens. I try to stop, but sometimes it's hard."

Garik lifted his leg, took a whiff, and nearly lost his nachos. And his leg was four feet from his nose.

"It doesn't smell too bad." Marco smiled. "Now if it gets wet—" he snickered "—that's a different story."

"And I'm supposed to wear this all night. Sheesh, Marco!"

The night sky had grown darker, and Garik realized he could no longer see the stars. Any light other than from the mall lighting came from buildings that over-looked the mall, and none of them were close.

A rumble started on the horizon, then spidery light-ning crawled across the sky. Dark circles appeared on the pavement, then more and more, until their pant legs were ringed with streaks of moisture.

And the smell. Garik knew that if he were hunted, no one would have any trouble locating him. Just take a whiff, locate the stinkiest thing around, and shoot him dead.

He might even welcome it if he had to wear these clothes much longer.

— 6 —

T

he rain battered the mall for a few minutes, a torrent of cold running off tables and sending the food kiosks into panic, covering their wares with giant tarps.

Then it was gone. The sky cleared, and the stars erupted in a cacophony of brilliant diamonds filling the cosmos overhead.

The marquee on the mall continued to blaze with the Ace of Holes logo. The water dripping from the sign gave it a futuristic look, sparkly, fracturing the lights into multiple tiny rainbows.

Alyna and John had found Garik and Marco. They

stood under the building, wet but not soaked. Others on the mall dripped, some twirling in the melee, their arms out, the release of a week's pent-up emotions bleeding out and running down the pavement like the water from the skies.

The elephant from the magic trick lifted its trunk, tossed its ears side to side, trumpeted.

"Looks like he's having fun." John pointed.

"*She's* having fun," Alyna suggested, giving him a jab in the elbow.

"How is it you're not cold?" The tall man's arms were uncovered, and Garik shivered.

"He's a walking heat pump." Alyna tittered. "It's the frog in his veins."

"Enough, Alyna," John cautioned.

"I never found Christian." Garik wanted to see him. He clenched his fists inside his coat pockets, creating bulbous half circles, and he wondered where Jantzen might be. Under the Tower had become standing room only when the sky was really falling, but the press of people was thinning. If the man was around, now would be the time to locate him, before everyone spread over the sixty-four blocks that made up the mall once again.

As Garik scanned the crowd, he caught Airman Vang a dozen tables over watching him. Airman Vang. As soon as Garik caught his eye, the Airman turned, lifted his nose, and began to speak to someone at his side.

Garik clenched his jaw. What am I to you, Airman Vang? A stone in your shoe? Someone who's achieved something you want to destroy? Whatever, it can't be good.

Jantzen was with Joseph Howard. Garik excused himself, saying he needed to speak with Jantzen, and he left them to brave the dripping skies or not, their choice. It became clear that Joseph wasn't there to enjoy the magic show. He held a long push broom with tight bristles. The end was wet, and an area behind him showed drying brush marks where a puddle of water had been worked into a drain.

Some peons are lower than other peons, Garik considered, feeling a swell of emotion for someone farther down the totem pole than him. He didn't get to think more on it, because a ruckus out on the open mall caught everyone's attention. The noise escalated, and swathes of people like waves of cloth billowed that direction, hiding whatever was going on. Jantzen was talking into his watch, and even with the distance and the noise, Garik heard him bark, "Now! Start the fireworks. Or people are going to notice the real show."

Jantzen looked up, saw Garik watching him, and shrugged. He mouthed, "Here we go again," or did Garik just imagine that's what he might have said? In either case, Jantzen's eyes turned a rich purple, deeper than Garik had seen before, and his clothes fell to the pavement, with only wisps of purple smoke coming out of the sleeves by the time Garik got there.

"He's done it again." Joseph grinned. "Likely will do it again, sometime."

"He'll want these." Garik gathered up his clothes. Fireworks on the mall began exploding, sending colored shadows dancing across the food court.

"Yep. Good seeing you." Joseph nodded, lowered his broom handle, and began pushing the next puddle of color-dappled water to the drain.

POOR MARCO.

Garik lay in bed with the darkness swirling around him, and he pictured the little lemur-enhanced man as he was wheeled off to the elevator to spend the night in the hospital, the reason the military presence was so strong on the mall during events.

Tonight, Marco had seen Justin arrive, and Garik guessed, with the memory of their discussion about Justin's spying and intimidation, the little guy hadn't been able to resist. He'd run up behind Justin, turned around, and scented him before running off.

John and Alyna were laughing, not expecting much of it, but Justin knew the aroma at first whiff. Marco was prone to marking locations all around the facility, and when he did, people knew exactly what they were smelling.

The bigger issue was that Marco could run between people, sometimes through their legs, or under their arms if they were holding hands, and certainly underneath tables and chairs.

Justin could do none of that, and he was blinded to everything except catching the little man and making him pay. What did not move out of his way was forced out of the way, and that included normal humans, hybridized humans, furniture, anything.

The people Justin slammed through often didn't see him coming, and he was gone by the time they picked themselves up. The person nearest got the blame, so Marco's little trick with Justin soon had a dozen fights spreading across the mall.

Justin had disappeared, but Marco hadn't been able to walk once Justin finished with him. Garik never did find Jantzen and left his clothing on the lobby desk on Level 1.

So, what were Justin's strong points? Why was he hybridized from a praying mantis? Garik wasn't sure he'd understand even if anyone told him.

What a night!

He turned, settled in, and listened to the gentle hum of the air from the overhead vent. Often it lulled him to sleep, especially when his thoughts ran away with his mind, causing him to toss and turn.

Tonight, he heard and smelled something that didn't belong. The odor was green and plantlike, the wild outdoors, an aroma he recognized from the gaming center.

Justin!

Garik sat up, working to pinpoint the smells and the sound, wishing he could see at night like a timber wolf. Then he would likely have eyeshine, and everyone else would know where *he* was!

The sounds had gone quiet, but the aroma remained.

"Justin?" he tested.

"Guilty." The voice was gritty in the darkness.

"Why are you in my bedroom?"

"Why did that little creep pee on me?" A big sigh. "Did I kill him?"

"They took him to the hospital, so I don't think so."

Garik rubbed his arms, his fingers gliding over prickles of fear. This conversation *in the dark* was totally surreal. He listened for an impending attack, the slightest movement of the mantis-adapted man.

"Can I turn the light on?" Garik wanted to see the attack when it came.

"Perhaps not." Justin breathed harder, almost a pant. "I'm roasted after this. You win, I lose."

The noise level from across the room increased tenfold, and Garik leaned over as quick as he could and slammed his hand on the light switch on his bedside table. The room erupted into a level of brilliance that assaulted his fear-laced sanity.

No Justin. Garik got out of bed slowly, his eyes searching for anyplace the man might be. In the next room, the front door stood ajar. Garik turned around, pressed his hand to the chair at his desk, and it was warm.

He lifted his hand and smelled of it. Green and soil. Chlorophyll and bacteria.

He wondered how Justin had gotten into his room, and even more, he puzzled how he had gotten out so quickly.

It was frightening what that man could do.

GARIK STUDIED the bearded man across from him in the break area. Half-finished sandwiches and individual bags of chips tumbled across the low table between them like a rocky beach after a storm, with paper napkin seafoam decorating the lot. After the situation on the mall the previous evening, Garik had expected their lunch to be postponed. Jantzen had asked if they could do a light meal in the break room, and he readily agreed.

Now he wrestled with whether to mention Justin being in his bedroom during the night.

Garik took a sip from a canned soda. Several of the tables had been filled earlier, people catching a late snack instead of breakfast, not unusual on the morning after a mall event, but like a wave on the shore, most had washed away when Jantzen arrived.

It seemed to Garik that the purple mist vanishing act set Jantzen apart from the crowd as much as Justin's combative anger drove people from him.

"I checked on Marco this morning." Garik wanted

to break the ice into last night.

"And?" Jantzen leaned back.

"You always want me to evaluate things, don't you?" Answer a question with a question. Don't give away everything you know. I'm learning, Jantzen.

"Yes." The dark-haired man studied him, his purple-flecked eyes pulling Garik inside.

"Okay." Garik looked away. He still wasn't strong enough to play games with the man. "Marco will be okay. Maybe," and he glanced at Jantzen with a grin, "Justin should have done more. Marco might have learned a lesson."

"Oh?" A smile cracked one side of Jantzen's face.

"Marco said that as soon as he's out of that bed they have him tied up in, he's going to mark Justin's other leg."

Jantzen laughed. "And you see what I deal with every day."

"What about Justin?" The question just came out. Last night Justin had sounded almost contrite. *"I'm roasted after this. You win, I lose."* Didn't he understand? This wasn't about winning or losing. This was about making the best of the hand they were dealt.

Even if they hadn't chosen to play the game and had been drafted in anyway.

"Is that sympathy I hear?" Jantzen leaned forward, lifted his can, took a sip, and replaced it before leaning back again, likely to give himself time to think. "Justin and I were once . . . good friends. I had my, um, alterations done first, and I didn't expect Justin—"

Garik watched Jantzen's face, his eyes. Not the purple, but the way he held them, looking off to something that was gone and couldn't be called back again.

"He did this without telling you, didn't he?"

"Yes." Jantzen's eyes cut to Garik. "I would have told him no, but then, recovery was longer for those of us who served as the early templates, and I didn't know until after it was done."

"And you feel sorry for him."

"I feel sorry for you—"

"Don't say that." Garik felt something hard rise up. He didn't like what they'd done, but he didn't want sympathy, not ever.

"I apologize. That sounded like pity, and that's not what I meant. For what you lost, for the things you can never have again."

"Why not? Why can't I have them back?" Garik sank into his seat in frustration, his throat raw with emotion. "I haven't changed. I'm still me. What's different? Nothing. Even this is coming back." He grabbed a handful of his hair, and he pulled at it. It was grown enough that he could do that.

"Yes, it is." Jantzen smiled and stood. "Have you been back to Level 5 since that first night?"

"You know I haven't. It still gives me nightmares."

"Do it. Today. I'll be spending some time with

Christian this afternoon."

"Christian?" Garik sat up, interested. "Last night, he didn't show. Then with the fighting, everything went sideways. Can I go with you?"

"Visit Level 5 first. Will you do that? Christian and I have some things we need to cover. You will understand better if you do as I ask."

Garik stood, his face growing hot. "What? You do this all the time, not tell me stuff. You don't trust me? I thought we were friends." Garik fought the emotions about to flood his face and shame him.

"Just visit Level 5. You won't regret it." Jantzen glanced at the table and sighed. "I'll send someone to clear this away."

"I'll do it," Garik grumbled after the man was gone.

He wasn't sure if his answer meant he would visit Level 5 or clear the table, but if he cleared the table, he could postpone his visit to Level 5, so that was where he started.

— 7 —

arik smashed the Level 5 on the elevator's control panel and watched the doors close him in.

What was he doing? He closed his eyes, leaned his head back against the wall, and let his thoughts fall into themselves, pulling him into a black hole of memories.

Marisa. Halo Sunchaser's passkey in her hand. She couldn't have known what would happen. He couldn't either. Would he have run to join her if he had?

Yes. Friends don't let friends go into danger, even of their own making, without standing by their side.

The doors opened, and the clean, bright light of the

bottom level of the Tower's basements washed into the tight, steel box. The memory of standing in this spot with Marisa and wondering if Gunther Diehl would walk up, tell them they were in the wrong location, and politely escort them to a suitable exit wiped away the months he had been trapped in the maw of the Corona Tower.

A rising surge of longing washed over him for Marisa's face, for sitting with her on the roof of their apartment building, visiting her at the flower shop, her laughter when his thoughts carried him away, and her reminding him that she was talking to him.

The sounds of the creatures in the cages on Level 5 filtered into the elevator. The door dinged as if to say, "Going up! I'm headed up!" and he moved forward, stepping in its way. He tried not to look into the cages, rather checking right and left while deciding where to go. He gripped his passkey. It now took him anywhere but to the food court, except during events. It was his lifeline back upstairs. He didn't want to be trapped here.

A worker in a white smock appeared from the end of a bank of cages pushing a cart. Garik froze, hearing those words from so many weeks ago. *"Hey, you!"* He expected to hear, "What are you doing here?"

Instead, the man raised a hand, called out, "Hello. We're expecting you," and began to walk his direction.

"I'm Garik." Fear gripped him, despite the man's

greeting. The BolaWrap hitting his legs, the feeling of falling, his head smashing into the floor. "Jantzen said—"

"We know. This way." He reached out a hand. He was already moving, Garik's guide through the basement. "Avery Isken. Normally I'm in the labs up on Two, but we all rotate to Five to help with the animals at least twice a month. I didn't make it to the event last night. I was down here covering for Nataly Jago. Have you met her?"

Garik shook his head.

"No reason why you should. I hear something happened during the event—that's why Justin's here. It's a shame, but he would have made it down here sooner or later. It happens with his kind."

His kind? Garik didn't know how to respond.

"Hey, you've arrived at feeding time. I've got the rest of that cart and one more to go. If you're still around, there'll be dinner tonight. You can stay and watch if you want."

"Stay and watch if I want," Garik repeated, repulsed. Was that what Christian would become, an animal to these people? Visited at feeding time, then locked away until the next feeding?

"We have a fresh shipment in, rhesus monkeys. Really cute." Avery glanced at him expectantly, then he shrugged. "Find me when you leave if you think you might. This is it. Take the third door on the right."

They stopped at a dividing wall with double glass doors separating the cages from a softly lighted corridor on the other side. The doors whooshed aside, and fresh-smelling air tumbled over them.

"Third on the right." Garik wasn't sure if he was asking for confirmation or putting off the inevitable. In either case, this was more Level 2 than the experimental operating theater he'd expected.

"Yes. Once people make it here, they don't get many visitors. I wasn't aware you two were friends. Shows you never know." Avery turned and his feet were loud on the hard floor.

Friends? Visitors? What about Christian? Garik had been under the impression he would be sliced up and offered to the latest participant in the human-hybrid program.

He stepped inside and felt the air change as the doors closed behind him. He remembered the way the air had tumbled over them. He turned to look and knew the doors were hermetically sealed. Positive air pressure prevented anything out there from getting in here. It made sense.

He knocked at the third door, mystified. Justin would make it down here sooner or later? What did they want to harvest from Justin? An extra set of joints? He shivered and knocked again.

"I've eaten. Go away." Justin, yelling.

"Good. Then you won't eat me," Garik yelled back.

"What are you doing here?" The door cracked slightly, revealing a darkened room.

"To see you, I think. Jantzen sent me." Garik looked back at the glass doors, wishing more than ever he hadn't come.

"Idiot." Justin slammed the door.

"Do you want me to go?" Garik closed his eyes and leaned his forehead against the door. It was cold.

"No." The sound of a chain being undone, and the door released. "Come in."

Garik pushed the door wide, forcing it into the gloom, and saw Justin disappearing into the depths.

At least he thought it was Justin. It was *something*. If it was Justin . . . Garik's picture of his own future turned upside down.

"SO, WHAT did you expect when you came down here?" Justin growled, a seething cauldron of animosity. Within the growl, a new clicking noise that Garik didn't recognize.

"Not you." The space was living quarters of a sort, though of a temporary kind. The darkness gave it a forbidding cast. "Why no lights?"

"You can't see, can you?" A rough laugh. "Ask Christian. You will soon enough."

"I don't get it. See what soon enough?" *Jantzen, why did you send me down here?* Garik would walk out, but the man had wanted him to discover something.

"Me, this room, you, everything. You don't think who you are right now is all you'll become, do you?"

"I don't know what to think. No one tells me anything." Jantzen had, though, perhaps without meaning to. *I don't know which changes are accelerating initially.*

"I'm part mantis, bred for my lack of fear. I'll tackle any opponent, no matter the size."

"That, I know." Garik had fought him.

"They haven't found anyone better, but I'm not their super soldier."

"Super soldier." Garik heard himself repeating Justin, and he didn't care. Jantzen had said something similar.

"Yeah. I'm too obvious, and I'm still changing."

"Still changing." That could explain what Garik had seen when he followed Justin into the room.

"You like to repeat people, don't you?" Justin laughed, adding a click at the end. "I used to do that when I was coming to grips with a new concept, especially one I didn't want to accept. I guess you need to see so you can get your head around this. By the way, I'm glad the little shrimp will be okay."

"Lemur." Garik wasn't certain he wanted to see.

"Lemur, schlemur. He was a foot taller when he started. Has anyone told you that?"

They hadn't. Julia flashed into Garik's head. She was tall, and she was part boa constrictor. They grew to massive lengths. How tall would she be eventually?

He pictured himself as wolf boy. Hairy ears, bushy eyebrows, and mitts like Christian's. It was too much to take in.

Just when he was ready to curl up and wish it all away, Justin said, "Surprise," and turned on the lights.

It was worse than Garik had imagined.

JUSTIN WAS bare from the waist up. His head wasn't much different, perhaps larger eyes. It was his torso that no one could miss.

"It's better when I have on my coat." Justin shifted position, and he stood. "It irritates my back." He turned. His back was more elongated, but the real difference was in the bulges running down his spine.

"What's happening?"

"Well, it seems mantises can fly." Justin smirked. "And that's becoming me. Not what I wanted to be able to do."

"So, wings in there. They are still growing, right?"

"My arms, too. Did you notice? Popeye." He held them in front of him. The sections between his human elbows and his shorter forearms had thickened, like the massive front legs of the insect he was modeled on. "I don't know . . . I'll take that back. *They* don't know how much longer I'll be able to stay here."

"This happened all of a sudden?" Garik thought of himself. How much warning would he have?

"No. I've been hiding it as best I can. You've seen my duster."

"I thought as much, but not that it was getting worse." Would John one day hop everywhere he went, Joanie require a saltwater pool, or Marco . . . it dawned on him. "Marco will continue to become more lemur-like, won't he?"

"And end up here eventually."

"And?" Like, what would happen? Would Marco also be "harvested" for his DNA-enhanced attributes?

Justin shrugged, but whether he didn't know or didn't want to say wasn't clear.

"Christian—" Now it was clear that the man had begun to shed more heavily, and his hands—all of him—had become more hound-like than ever. "Does it happen to everyone?"

"They've made progress. Your chances, perhaps, are better, if they were careful."

Garik understood why Jantzen had insisted he visit down here. Jantzen could have explained, but that wouldn't have satisfied Garik. Now, he understood at least the tip of what Christian might have to face and why he was being reassigned to the lowest level in the research facility.

"Will they let you continue to live here?"

Justin moved to the small kitchenette in the corner, and he rummaged in the fridge before pulling out a cardboard container. It was unlabeled. He stabbed a straw into the top. It was blood-red when he took a sip.

"Why do you think I gave all of you those recordings?" Neutral, not attacking.

"We didn't know. You planned to turn us in, we thought, but I don't think you did."

"I was angry." Justin nestled into the couch, avoiding pressing his back against anything hard. "But I wouldn't have turned you in."

"We weren't planning anything to do with you. Why would you be angry?"

"Now you're getting it." Justin's voice grew thick, laced with emotion. "You *didn't* include me."

"Why is that a problem?" Say it, man, or bug, or whatever you are!

"Are you stupid, too?" Justin lashed out. "I'm surrounded by idiots."

"No, I'm not stupid. I'm seventeen, I should be in high school right now, and I've been kidnapped to be a part of whatever you people are doing down here. I don't understand any of this." Garik felt the room jump ten degrees.

"You didn't volunteer?"

"Don't *you* listen? Or are *you* stupid? I fell into all this—" literally "—and I want to go home. I'm told that's impossible. The best I can do is try to help Christian escape."

"And I want to be part of that." Justin flexed his arms, revealing more strength in them than his thin torso might suggest. "I can help. Is it a deal?"

"I have to ask everyone else." Garik was sure Joanie and her friends would be grateful for all the help Justin could provide.

"I can appreciate that. Don't wait too long. We may not have much time."

Garik left the way he came. He kept his eyes averted from the cages, still unclear if Christian or Justin would someday be living in one of them. He kept his hand wrapped around his passkey, refusing to think about not being able to board the elevator and leave this place.

When the elevator doors closed, he felt his chest relax for the first time since the doors had opened.

Christian. Now Justin, and maybe Marco before long. Who else? He had started with wanting to save one man, and now it seemed like it was everyone who needed saved.

He was just a teenager. He hadn't even become a wolf yet, not that he could really tell. He was only now regrowing his hair.

What did they expect of him, to save everyone? He didn't even know how to save himself.

Sheesh!

— 8 —

The water in the pool swallowed Garik. He sank to the bottom, turned, looked up, let the rippling ceiling of the natatorium soak into his tortured thoughts. Legs and feet were icepicks across the surface, jabbing through the water, hands splashing, occasionally someone becoming a dolphin, flashing through the water, or a penguin, leaving trails of bubbles to mark their passage.

Workouts were better with Christian, the man tracking his progress with a timer, egging him on, calling, "Don't be a baby. You can do one more."

They had started this to give Christian more time,

and Garik hadn't seen what was occurring right before his eyes. The very thing that was Christian's conveyer belt down to Level 5 was still running, inexorably tugging him along, even as the man set out Garik's towel, added another weight to his weight machine, or helped him work out the kinks in sore muscles.

Whoever had programed Christian hadn't set an off switch in Christian's DNA, in his biobricks, in his sequence promoters. In the cellular primer that told his body how to absorb the characteristics of the wolfhound genes they wanted him to take on, they forgot that nature finds a way to bring survival characteristics to the forefront. Cherry picking this or that, precognition or intelligence, kindness or premediated focus that precluded an emotional connection with a perceived enemy was riding the knife edge of a blade, and it was easy to fall off. When you did, people got hurt. The good-hearted often died.

A team of researchers was running tests in the natatorium on aquatically adapted humans, most of whom didn't look especially aquatic, unlike Marina, Marisa's sister. Then, that was the point, to bring out the hybrid side without losing the human side.

It was a circus, a juggling act that could so easily go wrong. Justin's hands, whiplash quick, but one of his props had fallen out of the rotation, skittering off to the side, and Justin was scrambling to survive.

Marina, with her vestigial gills, and one side of her

body displaying scales and webbed fingers.

Marco, able to climb anything but clearly becoming more lemur than human. At least his intelligence was intact, if scenting people and getting beat up for it was a sign of intelligence.

Was Hector, adapted with a rat, a sign of what Garik would become? Would Garik begin howling at the moon, maybe even gnaw on meat scraps and bones?

Repeated splashing at the side of the pool drew his attention. It stopped, the surface cleared, and Giselle appeared, wavering through the water. She motioned for him to come to the surface. He nodded and waved, and he pushed off from the bottom.

"Yes?" he said, as he broke the surface, shaking the water from his hair. He drew in fresh air, and glancing around, he noticed that the team of researchers from earlier was gone.

"That's my thing, you know." She knelt on the rubberized surface surrounding the pool. "I'm the water woman, able to devolve and reconstitute myself."

"Oh?" Garik was several feet from the edge, and he moved his arms back and forth. The water was deeper than he was tall, and he didn't want to touch the coping. It was a connection with the real world, the one battering his life. In the pool, he was insulated, apart, just Garik for however long he could remain under.

It was motivation to remain submerged for a very long time.

"It sounds wonderful, like a comic character that can liquify herself at any time and become solid again." She touched the water, pushing her hand through the surface, and running her fingers back and forth. She sighed and laughed, a sad sound. "Not exactly."

"So?" Garik moved closer, curious, only now willing to touch the side of the pool with one hand, still separated, still aloof from the world, but making that tenuous connection for as long as the corrosive world around him maintained his interest. "What is it like, exactly?"

"You do know how a sea cucumber liquifies itself?" She pursed her lips playfully, clearly enjoying the question.

"I suppose it squirts out water."

"And all its organs." She grinned. "It has to regrow them later."

"You can do that?" He grimaced.

"You are so funny." She laughed. "The look on your face. I am half human, so no, I don't expel all my organs. I do have to rehydrate everything I expel. It's something better done in a body of water."

"The ocean, maybe a bathtub?" He grinned, enjoying her frankness for a change. "Or a pool?"

"That, too. Come out. Joanie got your message about Justin's offer. She's planned a meeting." She shifted her position as if to stand.

"Wait." Garik wrapped his hand around her wrist.

"Can you answer me a question?"

"If you ask the right one. First, my arm." The lower part of Giselle's arm suddenly bled water, shimmering with distorted light, and Garik's hand washed off, sending him backwards into the water. She smiled, jammed the arm into the water for a moment before lifting it and shaking it dry. "Good as new. Your question?"

"Are you still changing? You know, like—" It was important to Garik. Wolf boy, that sort of thing.

"Like Christian? No. Why?" She paused and said, "Oh, I get it. Let me see how to describe this. I'm second-generation hybrid. Christian is first—"

"Like Jantzen, and I think Justin, too." The realization hit Garik. What would Jantzen become? What was he hybridized with? Where had his accessory DNA been sourced? What could allow him to disappear into a cloud of purple mist?

"Yes, but every case is different, especially from the first generation. Trial and error in the initial modifications. Jantzen's was stable, or it has been so far."

"And Marco? What generation is he?" The man had changed just since Garik had known him.

"Marco is special. Intentional. Ask him about it, sometime. He loves to discuss it. Okay, I've answered your questions. Out." She stood.

"Wait. Me. What am I?" Second? Third? Or something else, intended to become a bizarre parody of a human being, only recognizable as human by what he once was? He had one hand on the side of the pool, and he floated with the water around his shoulders. The depths of the pool called to him. Her answer was important.

"We all want to know the answer to that question." She shrugged, gave him a teasing pucker and a wiggle of her fingers with one hand, and walked toward the door.

Garik pushed away and let the water swallow him once again. The answer was worse than not knowing. He looked around, noticing the lack of activity in the water. He swam upward, breaking the surface, and realized he was alone.

How long had he been down? Chill bumps erupted over him, tiny volcanoes of dread. He pushed toward the ladder, the water swirling behind him, a trail of bubbles telling where he was, where he wasn't, and that he soon would be no more.

Then what? Garik pulled himself from the water into the air, imagining himself as a sea creature taking its first steps on land, not having a clue that one day it would become elephants and birds and people and this place called Corona Tower.

That was just it. Garik had no clue. And now, it seemed, no one else did, either.

"NO, NO, NO. Justin is not welcome!" Marco Lopez

flicked his tail, and he grimaced. "Ow, that still hurts."

"Then don't do it." Julia cracked open a package of gum, pulled out a square, and offered it around before shrugging and returning it to a pocket.

"It's instinctive," Marco moaned, holding a part of his tail that had been shaved, a victim of Justin's aggressive response to his impulsive scenting trick on the mall. "You tell yourself to quit blinking and see how that works."

"Okay. I'm part boa, and constrictors don't have eyelids." She smacked her gum and grinned.

Alyna flexed her claws, chuckling, the soft sound of the knife-like keratin unsheathing and sheathing enough to run a chill down someone's back.

"What?" Marco glared at her. He was still bandaged in several places, and in others, his hair was only now beginning to regrow. "You see me, don't you?" He pointed to his injuries. "Justin did this. Totally uncalled for. Fry him, that's what I say."

"Enough." Joanie stood, her mohawk towering over her. "No trust. Prove otherwise." She pointed to the pile of mini flash drives on the table between them, one for each person present, and she pointed to Garik.

Garik considered his response. Jantzen had started this, used him as a messenger boy. He had sent him on a mission to understand Justin, and now Garik was championing a man who had once been his opponent, if not his enemy. In Justin's plea to help was an old connection between the two men. Garik didn't see it, but he could see how it affected his mentor. For that alone, he was willing to do this.

"Justin's changing—"

The room exploded. "Tell us something new." "Like everyone." "As if we aren't." "He knew what he signed on for." "Deal with it."

Garik gave it a moment to settle. "This is different. I don't think he will mind me telling, but you do realize mantises can fly?"

"I can shoot boiling water." Paolo held up one hand, showing his fingertips. "Any takers?"

Garik restarted. "Justin has boil-like places on his back. He tells me they are developing into wings. And his arms, if you haven't noticed, no longer look human."

When eyes turned toward Marco, he held up his hands and said, "What? I'm human where it counts." He made a fist and hit it twice on his chest.

Garik continued, "I'm learning each of us has been hybridized for a specific characteristic. I learned Justin's when I visited him. Before, I thought, mantis? What's that got that anyone would want? Sure, his arms are lightning fast, but people can see that coming. Justin said they really wanted him for his lack of fear at a bigger opponent. Nothing frightens him."

"He frightens me," Leigh whispered.

"And me," chimed in Giselle.

"See? Justin knows he's on the way out, and Christian—" everyone nodded in agreement "—and you, Marco—" bringing a frown from the man "—and who knows who else? Justin knows his anger issues, the changes he's been trying to hide the past months. That's why he made the recordings. He wants to be included, and that's the only way he knew to tell us."

"Appreciated." Joanie nodded at Garik, thanking him. "Anyone else?"

"If he's already on Level 5, how can he help?" Laura.

"Understood—" Joanie started, when Julia pointed her head at the door and froze. "Julia? A problem?"

"The door. Someone with bad news."

"Bad news?" Garik whispered to Paolo. "She can tell that?"

"Infrared. Stress elevates the body temperature."

The door shuddered, the knob rattled, and then it swung wide. John Carter fell into the room, with Amy Howe behind him. Panic painted his face.

"John?" Joanie invited him to share.

"It's Christian." John crumpled. Amy patted the side of his face.

"Your blood, John. Chill yourself down. You've allowed yourself to overheat." Looking around, she shrugged. "You didn't expect me, did you?"

"Obviously." Alyna's claws were out. "What do you know?"

"More than I've told. I want in, too."

"First, Christian." The one word was all Joanie needed to say.

"They've moved him—"

"Where?" Garik's mind skipped to every possibility. Level 5? He wasn't there when Garik was.

"Jantzen's had a big showdown with Halo. It's still going on—"

"I knew Halo was competitive, but this?" Laura's expression darkened, and she shivered. "Who next, us?"

"Where's Christian?" Garik said it louder than he intended, but it got the attention he wanted.

"Disappeared." John pulled himself to his feet. "He's no longer in the facility. That's what Jantzen and I have been doing, looking for him. When Jantzen discovered he was gone, he exploded all over Halo. Now, Weston's in it. There's no telling—" He took a deep breath and looked pale.

"Suck it up, frog boy," Amy said, patting his arm.

Garik was stunned. This news was as bad as it could get.

At least he hoped so.

— 9 —

I

have told you what I require."

Garik caught the words, the superior lilt that could only come from one person, Halo Sunchaser.

They weren't directed at him, and he couldn't see who she was speaking to, but the steel in her voice was of the tempered kind, beaten and honed to a knife-edge sharpness.

An electrified sword-cutting edge sharpness.

Garik shivered, glad he wasn't in the room. He stood outside the ajar door of the facilities management offices on Basement Level 2, where he had once waited while Jantzen had cleared the calendar with Rachel Prager for Garik to spend the day with him. The long rows of closed-off windows lining the corridor suggested a warren of rooms and no telling how many employees. There was no way to know who was receiving Sunchaser's tongue-lashing ultimatum.

After making his escape from Joanie's—*Christian, lost!*—Garik's head had spun. The corridors had been vast, blurred transitions from non-real space to the infinity of a failure where he had stumbled while guarding someone he had committed his life to protect.

Despair and despondency had transitioned to anger, though it was currently anger with no focus. Who did he blame? Halo Sunchaser? Marisa had worshipped her, or at least her electrified sword, and the woman had been kind enough to escort them on the beginnings of their much-anticipated tour of Corona Tower. Kevin Lee seemed to regard her as a near friend, or as much of a friend as someone as mysterious and powerful as Sunchaser could be. Garik had felt sorry for her when she had dropped everything—literally—when Weston Rodheimer had appeared at the beginning of the tour.

Who wanted to live in that kind of fear? Garik had Arik, his aunt's boyfriend, to contend with, so he understood.

"Halo," Garik recognized Rachel Prager's bright, efficient voice, "I am certain Jantzen wishes to cooperate with you fully and without reserve. He has not been in this office today. When I hear from him, I will pass on your message."

"I will follow through on this, Rachel. What happened this morning was unconscionable and highly inappropriate to a person in my position. I will not have my authority undermined for the sake of a failed project participant."

"Halo," another familiar voice, Weston Rodheimer, "Jantzen is not proven guilty of insubordination. He is technically your superior, so he has the right to question. We must resolve this with care."

"Don't lecture me, Weston. When my parents were killed in the South Africa race riots, they died as the result of cumulative disrespect that began as a disregard for authority. Bongani hasn't spoken to me since I left, but I accepted that insult from my brother rather than live with the racial inequities that took my parents from me. This is important to me."

"I understand, Halo." Rodheimer, again. "The situation today is far different. As a senator, Bongani must keep himself separate from his sister in North America. To do otherwise is political suicide. It is why we let no one know you are a successful part of our genetic modification program. You will have a chance to prove yourself to Bongani when we are allowed to publicize our success. Jantzen's situation is completely different. He supported Christian throughout his transition and was unprepared for the unexpected departure of his longtime friend—"

"Friend?" Sunchaser laughed bitterly. "Are you sure? I hear the tales. I suspect it was once more."

"It doesn't matter. Jantzen has supported our program and been key in most of our advances. He is second-in-command. I will not have him undermined without just cause."

The door clicked, closing completely, and Garik jumped at the metallic noise, thump, thump, that told of the locking mechanism falling into place. This was not a door his passkey would open, although he wouldn't try it even if it did.

His disappointment not to hear more of the conversation was put aside by his confusion. He remembered how Rachel had "arranged" for Jantzen to keep him out of harm's way after the broken mirror incident involving Devon, and he suspected she had been guarding her words with Sunchaser. She knew more than she was sharing. She had told Sunchaser that Jantzen hadn't been in *this* office today, not that she didn't know *which* office he might be in.

Garik considered where his mentor might be. Facilities management wasn't his only home base. He was a researcher and maintained offices in the research labs, and he was certain Jantzen frequented the research hospital, also, and likely had space set aside for his current projects there. Space was not at a premium in the five-story basement research complex, from what Garik could tell.

Garik hit the heel of his palm to his forehead, whispering, "Stupid, stupid Garik. Of course."

He glanced down the corridor, placing the locations of the underground elevators on his mental map. The floors got smaller the farther down they went, and not every elevator accessed where he needed to be. The main elevator was five city blocks away, if he followed the contours of the city above, and he didn't have his ZBoard with him. His apartment in Corona City was farther, and he wasn't sure where the closest access to additional motorized transportation was located.

He really should have spent more time memorizing the layout of the facility, or at least Level 2 where he lived. He felt so stupid, sometimes.

He could likely sprint to the elevator faster, anyway, as lately, since his track time with Christian, he was rarely out of breath, even after his most intense sessions. Long-distance runs were no longer a blip on his radar of things that seemed impractical or inconvenient.

Two people crossed the corridor at an intersection, one a dark-haired woman wearing normal street attire and carrying a sheaf of paperwork in the crook of her arm. She was talking to a man, slightly taller, who was on a handheld phone. He wore glasses and touted dark hair pulled back severely from his face. The man glanced at Garik, nodded, and looked away. The woman didn't seem to register Garik's presence at all.

Garik knew he would intersect people on his way, and he didn't want to raise questions. Sunchaser. She had been furious, and he didn't want it aimed at him. And Rodheimer? He was frightening, both in his size and his grip on power in the Tower.

At the first intersection of corridors, Garik slowed, looking carefully as he walked across, and only increasing his speed when he was sure he couldn't be seen. Two corridors had groups of people outside, one likely a meeting on a break, with the people wearing their names on lanyards around their necks, and the other workers in paint-spattered coveralls, obviously completing a remodeling project. The name plaque beside the door had been removed, leaving discolored paint and two screw holes.

By the time Garik reached the main elevator, he was running by instinct. He heard the voices before he saw the people, could tell by scent if he were meeting one, two, or more—only once surprised by a posse of eight, his sense of smell overwhelmed by sheer numbers—and found himself noting nooks and crannies for hiding and alternate routes he could take even though he wasn't required to use them.

It was the speed that was important, his surroundings blurring into a rainbow haze, using uncanny, wolf-like senses, although to Garik, he was just in a hurry, things sounded and smelled like they were supposed to, and he was making astounding progress.

He arrived at the elevator, grateful to find one of the two unoccupied, and he inserted his passkey. When the panel lit up, giving him permission to select Basement Levels 1-5—but not the food court or the upper levels of Corona Tower—Garik balled a fist and, with his knuckles, smashed the icon for Level 5.

There was only one place Jantzen could be that Sunchaser wouldn't think to look. He was certain he would find him there.

GARIK TWISTED the knob and fell with his shoulder against the door, trusting, hoping, but surprised to find it unlocked and sending it wide into Justin's temporary quarters. He was surprised to find it fully lighted.

"Jantzen? Justin?" He listened, his heart alight with anticipation, willing it to slow its pounding beat.

"Here, Garik." Jantzen, calling from deeper within.

"I knew you'd be here." Garik pushed into the space, to discover Justin face down and stretched along the floor. He wore only shorts, leaving his legs exposed. His shins . . . spurs?

"Forgive me if I don't look up." Jantzen knelt over Justin, with his back to Garik, working on the prone man's torso.

"Garik." Justin's arms were under his head, and he turned to look at Garik. He grimaced, and Jantzen paused, sat up, apologized, and leaned forward again.

Garik hadn't expected this, what appeared to be

surgery. Shouldn't this be happening in the hospital, Dr. Jamie or another of the trained staff?

"The best I can do," Jantzen said, pulling a towel from beside him and wiping his hands. "Perhaps the pain won't be so bad."

"What are you doing?"

"What I can." Jantzen turned to him. "You look like you're in a rush."

"It's Sunchaser." Garik could now see Justin's back. The swellings were larger and redder than before. A towel marked with yellow and red looked like Jantzen had been draining fluid from the wing nodules. Justin moved to sit up, placing one hand on the floor, bending his second arm joint backwards, and navigating to a sitting position.

"I'm okay," Justin said, shifting position to try to get comfortable. He called to Garik, "What about her?"

"She's—" He looked between the two men, sensing the moment as a slippery stone, and leaped. "She was in Rachel's office, and Rachel wouldn't tell her where you were."

Justin looked to Garik, smiled, and turned to Jantzen. "Rachel hasn't changed."

"No. What did you overhear?" Jantzen seemed pleased, but his eyes were tired.

"Everything, well, until the door closed. I don't think it's good. And Christian, what happened to Christian? No one knows."

Jantzen seemed to deflate. "I was too late. He's no longer here."

"That's what John said, but where? Can we rescue him?"

"Patience, Garik. Perhaps. I'm working on that."

"There's no time, Jantzen. Now. I promised—" Garik felt his chest tighten, and he fought his face. "I can't let him down. He's a part of us."

"See?" Jantzen turned to Justin, nodding, speaking quietly as though confirming something. "Protect the pack above all else."

"Finally, success?" Justin, in a whisper.

"It's too early to tell. Perhaps."

"I'm right here," Garik barked. "Sheesh, you'd think I'm deaf."

"Maybe not too early." Justin chuckled, and he shifted position and groaned.

"Still painful? There's not much more I can do."

"I'm fine. Talk to the boy."

Boy. Garik had bested the man in the ring, the same way Jantzen had bested him in his fight with Alyna. He tempered his irritation with his old mantra, *my hands, my mind*, convinced that Sunchaser's backstabbing needed to be shared.

"Yes, Garik. What did you find out?" Jantzen made his way to the sofa and dropped.

"She's looking for you. She was talking about her brother in South Africa—"

"That again." Jantzen leaned his head back and closed his eyes. "Halo is jealous, but she has no foundation for it. I hope this doesn't go over your head, Garik, but she once thought we could be together, and that wasn't going to happen. Now, anyone I get close to, she tries to undermine, part of the reason I've kept my distance from you."

"I don't get it. What do I have to do with you and her?" Garik respected Jantzen. Wasn't that a good thing? He was so confused his head spun.

"I'm sure there's more to it—"

"She wants in Weston's favor. That's the more," Justin interrupted. "If Weston can bring her sick grandmother into the country—"

"Our DNA therapy can't . . . isn't designed for repair of cellular organisms. Halo knows that. It only modifies them." Jantzen shook his head.

"Try to convince a desperate granddaughter of that."

"Okay," Garik wailed, no longer caring about Sunchaser's grandmother. "Us, what are we going to do about us? If Christian's gone, we have to get Justin out. How can we do that?"

"He's your proof, your success. I'm telling you." Justin stretched one foot and pushed on Jantzen's leg.

"I can't be a success if you two don't help me!"

Jantzen shook his head and groaned.

— 10 —

I remember that Ms. Sunchaser was planning on a trip to South Africa for a martial arts competition." Garik looked up at the mirror spanning the top of the elevator, his face looking back at him, next to him the top of Jantzen's head, and the man's shoulders hiding the rest of his slender shape. Jantzen's arm reached to insert his passkey to engage the control panel.

Garik's shoulders had widened from his time in the gym with Christian. He now went alone. He moved his arms, certain his chest in the reflection had filled out. His lower body? That, he couldn't find in the mirror.

"And she returned, her carved tribal mask in one hand and a trophy in the other." Jantzen pushed the up button, and the doors closed. "Why?"

"She seemed so normal. When I first met her, I thought she was about to eat me alive, like a bird of prey. Then, she seemed concerned that she wouldn't do well in the competition, and she became human."

"Yes, she can do that. I fell for it once, but don't trust it. The human part. She will eat you."

Garik shivered, a cold chill feeding on his self-confidence and bravado. Soon, he would have neither.

"What will you do if—" If she finds you, Garik was about to ask, but as he was speaking, the elevator stopped, the filtered and perfumed air flowing from the vents failed, the lights surrounding the top of the compartment went dark, and the backlight panel around the controls clicked on.

"Not now, Hector." Jantzen looked up at the lights and sighed. "Focus, man."

Jantzen's watch dinged, and he slipped an earbud into one ear. "I'm in the elevator. I told you to wait on my signal. Focus, Hector. I told you I would let you know when to cut the power."

Cut the power? Garik had imagined Jantzen as a team player, even if today had suggested he might be in the process of being voted off the team. Was he planning an insurrection? If so, Garik was totally for it. Maybe this was his chance to make a difference, to save someone, to stand up with the big boys and be counted.

"What's happening on the main level?" Jantzen, again, at the panel, pushing buttons, and he inserted his passkey. The backlight panel became a viewscreen, and Jantzen scrolled through several images with a control Garik couldn't see. They showed the area just outside the elevator on the various basement levels, into the food court, and the Tower's main lobby. Mostly it looked normal, suggesting only the elevator they were on was compromised and not the building, itself.

"What do you mean, when can I get Justin there?" Jantzen frowned. "I'm on the elevator, Hector. Can you give me power just to the main car? Yes, the big breaker. It may be black."

The lights overhead flickered and came on. The air remained silent. Jantzen shrugged at Garik.

"You were supposed to be off before Hector cut the power. Now, we're against the clock. I've got override control of this elevator, and I've cut access from the outside. The second one is still operational, but as soon as it becomes obvious I have an override on this one, an alarm will sound, and this goes belly up."

"Okay, what goes belly up?" Rescue for Justin? Garik wanted to help, but how could Justin get away? He'd never pass for human. He was growing *wings*, for heaven's sake.

"I'm meeting with Kevin Lee—"

"To help Justin escape?" The elevator car swirled

with possibilities. Garik had no idea the martial arts instructor knew about the goings-on in the basements of the Corona Tower.

"We hope. Our planning isn't that far along, yet. Our first step is to see if we can get him away from the building. Every vehicle Corona Corporation has is tagged, logged, and inspected entering and exiting. We need a car no one will suspect."

"Kevin's." Garik pictured the man showing up for private lessons with Halo Sunchaser, or maybe for his visits to the different recreational activities in the Tower. Perhaps he had received special permission to park in the garage.

If Kevin's car came in or out, no one would see a need to inspect it. He was there to instruct Halo Sunchaser. What could be more innocent than that?

"I was meeting him after I dropped you off. Now, you're with me." The car began to move, heading up.

"That might be problematic. Kevin knows me. I'm supposed to be back in Russia." Even as he offered the warning, Garik was calculating how he could get a message back to Marisa and one to his aunt. If they knew, if they came looking for him, he was certain he could be rescued. They would have to let him go.

"That is a problem, I agree." Jantzen lifted his arm, placed his hand on his forehead, thinking, and he worked his jaw. "It can't be helped now. Can I count on you?"

Garik wanted escape, not to work with Jantzen. Yet, the man had become a mentor, a friend of sorts, if in a limited way. He didn't want to abandon what he'd agreed to help him do, but he also didn't want to abandon this opportunity for escape. His mind raced, searching for a way to do both, to begin his escape, and to not let down the people he'd come to share his life with.

He couldn't come up with a plan to do both.

"I need an answer, Garik, before I open this door."

"You're helping Justin?" A thousand needles shredded Garik's stomach.

"Yes." Jantzen held his hand over the door's controls.

"And Marco, too?"

Jantzen raised his eyebrows. "If he asks, certainly."

"What do you need me to do?" His eyes burned. He was in the cell, closing the door, and locking it after him. Why, why, why?

"Nothing. Just let me talk." Jantzen hit the open button, left his passkey in the door, and stepped through when it slipped sideways. "Follow me."

Garik stared at the passkey. Two feet away, and he had his freedom. *Two feet away!* His mind churned with images of the past months, and one kept coming to him, lying in his bed in the darkness listening to Justin say, *"I'm roasted after this. You win, I lose."*

"I'm sorry, Marisa." Garik's eyes burned as he stepped outside of the elevator to find himself in the polished foyer leading to the pool. Through the glass door, a woman in a green suit sat to the side reading a magazine in a woven rush chair, and a man with slender legs and a round belly lowered himself into the water.

"Kofi!" Jantzen greeted the pool boy, Kofi Mandela, with a raised hand. "I believe Kevin Lee is scheduled to use the pool today."

"Yes, Mr. Hefferly. After his session with Ms. Sunchaser. He hasn't yet arrived."

"Have you heard why?" Jantzen seemed surprised.

"Ms. Sunchaser had business this morning, and she scheduled Kevin a half-hour late. Garik? Is that you?" Kofi smiled broadly. "We were told you had returned to Russia. I'm glad to see you back. If you wish to use the pool with Kevin, I can offer you a suit. You have filled out. Perhaps a larger size than last time?"

Garik didn't know how to answer, and he turned to Jantzen for help.

"Yes," Jantzen said. "For both of us, if you don't mind, Kofi. Thank you, and yes, a larger size for my friend."

"Give me a moment while I retrieve them." Kofi stepped through a narrow door and it closed after him.

"We're swimming?" Garik's thoughts were entangled in running away, finally free; and following through on his responsibilities to those in the research program. And swimming? What had happened to urgent?

"Kofi needs to think so. He's returning. Quiet."

"These should work." Kofi offered Jantzen two towels and two suits.

"Thank you." The couple still lounged by the pool, and Jantzen said, "We will wait on Kevin in the changing room, and Kofi?"

"Mr. Hefferly, yes?"

"I'm leaving that elevator locked open. I know that's unusual, but this is special. Please see that it's undisturbed."

"Certainly, Mr. Hefferly."

Jantzen nodded for Garik to follow, and they entered the changing rooms. The space smelled comfortably clean, with the odor of mangos filtering through the air. When the door closed, he set the suits and towels on a counter and dropped to a bench. He leaned his head back and closed his eyes.

"So? What now?" Garik's muscles told him to run. His head said the elevators had him trapped on this floor. Perhaps with Jantzen's . . . then he remembered Gunther Diehl resetting the passkeys with Marisa's thumb on Halo Sunchaser's. Jantzen's wouldn't work for him even if he could get to it before Jantzen could catch him. He also remembered the night of the fight between Justin and Alyna. When Justin had gone for blood, Jantzen had evaporated and been across the games room before Garik could blink.

It wasn't likely that Garik could outrun the DNA-enhanced man.

"Kevin's cooperation is key. Maybe this is good, you being here. He knows me, but even more importantly, he knows you from outside, and—"

"You haven't talked with him?" Garik was appalled. He was trading his freedom for a possibility? "I thought you had this sorted out with Kevin, whatever it is you're planning."

"Nothing is ever sorted out, my young friend, and this?" He looked around the inside of the changing rooms. "Opportunity, that's all. I didn't intend to involve you, not until after I spoke to Kevin, and perhaps not then. I might be creating more trouble for myself than I expect, and I expect a lot. Weston will be furious."

The door flew open, startling the two men, and Kevin called out, "Garik? You in here?"

"Yah!" Garik grinned, surprised at the warmth in the words. He expected to be a nonentity to the man. He'd only known him a short time before he had disappeared.

"Hey, you moron. I just get to know you, and you vanish for months. How's Russia?" He grinned. "Mr. Hefferly, did you know this guy refused my invitation to train at Ai Kee!?"

"That's nice, Kevin."

"Have you seen Marisa since you've been back? She must be thrilled. Man, you leaving took it out of her. I hope you're back for good."

"Yeah, about that, um, Kevin," Garik started, looking to Jantzen. The mention of Marisa was a knife.

"Kevin, before you and Garik get too touchy-feely, I need to ask you a very big favor. Are you parked in the garage?"

"Sure, Mr. Hefferly. Ms. Sunchaser validates my parking. Is that okay? I was assured it would be fine on the days I give her lessons here at the Tower."

"Will you rent me your car for the night?" Jantzen pulled out his wallet. "Any amount."

"Rent you my car . . ." Kevin frowned. "Why?"

"My reasons, and if you're worried about damages, I'll guarantee it's returned in perfect condition. If any damage occurs, and you can be the judge, I'll have it repaired to your satisfaction."

"I, um, don't have any plans to use it tonight. What time can I pick it up tomorrow?"

"Will the afternoon do?" Jantzen had pulled out several large bills, and as he talked, he kept adding to them.

"Before you give me all that, I didn't drive my car today."

Jantzen hesitated. "Can you bring it in and leave it later?"

"No, that's not it. I'm in the Center's truck, well, transport van. If you need a car . . ." Kevin shrugged.

Jantzen held out the wad of cash, and Kevin

grinned. A knock at the door startled them.

"Yes?" Jantzen called.

"I'm sorry, Mr. Hefferly. I know you said not to let the elevator be disturbed, but Mr. Rodheimer and Ms. Sunchaser are here. They are demanding to see you."

"Thank you, Kofi." He held out his hand to Kevin. "Keys?"

"Oh, of course." Kevin placed them in his hand. "Good to see you, Garik, and thanks, Mr. Hefferly. I know you'll take good care of the van."

"Of course, Kevin. I appreciate your cooperation." On the way out, Jantzen's face lost its luster.

"Is this your big trouble?" Garik didn't need big trouble.

"We'll see, but likely."

"Should I let you do all the talking?"

"Halo may do it for us. Just hope that Weston takes my side. That's our best bet."

Garik had his own opinion there. He intended to keep his mouth shut and look as small as he could.

— II —

hen they stepped into the pool's lobby, Sunchaser was pacing, and seeing them, she seemed to grow four inches, anger swirled around her like windblown debris, and she erupted in a violent assault. Her wrap encircling her hair vibrated with pent-up energy.

"Finally, I put it together. This is the boy that helped that girl steal my passkey, Weston, and here he is, with Jantzen, roaming the tower unsupervised. The lost passkey was not my fault, and this proves it. Something has to be done."

Rodheimer, massive even next to the towering

Sunchaser, darkened, his thoughts tumbling across his face like a storm cloud, and he growled, "Jantzen, are you aware of this?"

Jantzen sighed and cut his eyes to Garik. His shoulders drooped. "It's likely. The timeframe fits."

"He admits it." Sunchaser's words seemed to boil as they hit the air. "If I had not been pulled away to South Africa, I would have made this connection before. Jantzen, once more you use your position to undermine mine, working behind my back when I am away. Did you arrange for that girl to abscond with my passkey? And to think, it was your suggestion that we not retain her, also. What are you planning now? I was right to fast-track Christian's removal. I can see it now, this boy. Weston, your number two has plans afoot, and they will not bode well for the project. You must act now."

"I admit I was furious this morning. Christian's removal was unexpected. I can only apologize." Jantzen glanced to Kofi, who had faded into the equipment room with the door cracked. It slipped shut. Kevin had not appeared, likely avoiding the confrontation.

"The boy?" Rodheimer's voice was the rumble of a train track in the night. "What explanation do you offer for his presence?"

"Coincidence, only. We were in the elevator at the same time—"

"And he locked it out, for a quick escape, I'm

certain. His passkey is the inescapable evidence. Keep that in mind, Weston." The air around Sunchaser vibrated with energy.

"Is Halo wrong?" Rodheimer, for a moment, seemed hopeful.

"Not wrong, just that my actions have been misconstrued. Let's meet tomorrow, you and me. Invite Halo if you wish. We can work this out, Weston."

Garik recognized what Jantzen was doing, playing for time to get Justin out of the research facility. He offered a prayer, but he also looked to the elevators, wondering if he could get to one and whether his own passkey would operate it from here.

Rodheimer turned to Sunchaser. "What do you suggest, Halo?"

"Restrict him to levels two and four, for a start. He has demonstrated his disregard for your position and mine. He thinks more of those that fail to perform satisfactorily than he does the success of this program. He has made a mockery of my authority and yours. Today is a perfect example, bringing one of his pets up here with him."

"Jantzen, are you taking this in? I have overlooked much for the sake of our history together and your contributions to the program. I forgive people when they fail me, but I expect them to make it right. This is not making things right. You are a brilliant researcher, but I cannot overlook this. I agree with Halo."

"I am fully supporting our research, Weston. My results speak for me. I can hardly work efficiently if you restrict my mobility about the facility. If we can't meet tomorrow, perhaps Rachel can schedule a better time." He smiled hopefully.

"Weston, I expect results, not for this to be put off again. I will not have this man continuing to flaunt my authority, and yours, too. You must support me in this." Sunchaser's voice had gone ragged with fury.

"Understood. Jantzen," Rodheimer turned to him, "I'll expect you to restrict yourself to your apartment until we get this resolved. I will retain your passkey for the foreseeable future."

Jantzen's eyes narrowed and his shoulders stiffened. His pupils glowed purple, and Garik tensed, waiting for the man to evaporate into purple mist. Nothing could hold him. He would be gone. It was an exciting moment, until the impact of his own situation left him flash-frozen in despair. Jantzen's escape would mean leaving him behind. He tried to catch the man's attention, and he shook his head, pleading. *Don't leave me, Jantzen.*

"I will do as you ask." Jantzen relaxed, giving in. Garik's head swam with relief.

"Also, the boy." Sunchaser turned her eyes to him, fire flying. "He is complicit and uncooperative, and for that, a failure. He must be restricted. Better, reassign him to Level 5."

Garik's knees nearly gave way. He was certain he would vomit if he had anything to expel.

Rodheimer looked from Jantzen to Garik, as if evaluating the success Garik had exhibited in contrast to the insubordination of being discovered in the Tower with Jantzen. He seemed to come to a decision.

"I will arrange it in the morning. Airman Vang will escort you both to your quarters."

Airman Vang moved forward from the shadows with hand restraints ready. He slapped them together noisily. Garik was certain the man grinned.

And he thought things were as bad as they could get. Never, never think that, he reminded himself. You will be disappointed every time.

Then the restraints were pulled tight, and he was yanked forward, with what little freedom he'd earned once more stolen from him.

GARIK LAY in the darkness, his head a vice, his brain squeezed, and his thoughts erupting in clumps of misery that spattered the walls with despair.

Locked! His door, his passkey useless!

He wondered why they hadn't taken it away, had tried it in his door, only to understand. They wanted him to be crushed with false hope. Well, it was working.

The sound of metal shearing, of voices whispering furtive things, drew him up and pulled him to the living room. Light leaked from around the lock on the door.

Hope? Did he dare? Or was this his end, Sunchaser sending someone to collect him, banishing him to Level 5 in the dark of the night, or worse, eliminating him altogether? Was that a possibility? He suspected it was.

The thump of metal separating from metal, and the door released. Garik slapped a switch, flooding the room with brilliance, and he backed away, prepared to fight, whatever they might come at him with. When the door swung back, Alyna Lindberg stood, held her hand in front of her, blew on her claws, and retracted them with a grin.

"Like a hot knife through butter." She winked at Garik.

"Or through molten steel." Julia Cantos leaned in behind her. "Inside, Alyna. I can sense someone coming."

They moved inside, and Julia fell against the door, holding it to. She shrugged and explained, "You don't have a latching mechanism any longer, thanks to Alyna. Sorry."

"I, um, what's—" Garik stumbled out the words. "You can cut metal?"

"Not the important question," Alyna suggested, "but yes. The important thing is what to do with you. Did Weston or Halo find out about the car?"

"Kevin's?" He shook his head. "Jantzen already had the keys, and it didn't come up. And it's not a car. It's a transport van."

She looked at Julia and nodded. "Even better. Did Jantzen give you the keys?"

"No."

"Then we hope they didn't search him and take them away. We'll leave that to Leigh and Paolo. If they did, perhaps Giselle can help. We'll have to have water, though. She'll need it if she's going to get inside the van."

"Justin is getting rescued?" Garik felt hope return.

"Yes." Alyna sighed, stretched her neck, and looked up and down Garik's pajamas. "You, young man, need clothes. How quickly can you dress?"

"What sort?" He grinned. He was being offered the chance to help. He was certain.

"Outside clothes, the warmest you have. Now."

He turned, excitement racing through him, and caught the doorway with his shoulder. He called back, "I'm okay," and he leaped for his closet.

As he dressed, he overheard the women talking.

"Has everyone been notified?"

"Marco thought he could do it by the time we got Jantzen out."

"And Justin?"

"He's mine, if Paolo can't manage." Garik overheard the swish of Alyna's claws extending and retracting. "If that kid in there will get the rocks out and get back in here."

"I heard that," Garik called. "I'm not deaf!"

He heard Julia chuckle and say, "Jantzen said he could do that."

Then their voices fell too low for him to overhear.

JULIA LED them, a passkey in her hands. Her ability to sense metabolic heat by infrared—the adaptation she had received from her constrictor DNA—kept them from being surprised by people along the way to the parking garage.

Garik was the one they were concerned about, although no one outside of Rodheimer, Sunchaser, and Airman Vang would likely think anything of him roaming the facility. Still, when someone approached, Garik pulled a hood over his head and kept his face averted. He wore a backpack filled with water bottles. Even with the extra weight, he could have done the journey faster and with less fuss if he knew the details of what was happening, but that was wishful thinking.

They worked their way to the research labs, and Alyna pulled out a second passkey. She held it up and whispered, "Let's hope this works. If not," and she flexed her claws and grinned. She inserted it into the panel by the door, and after a moment, it turned green. The locking mechanism thumped twice, and Alyna placed her hand on the latch. A twist, and it swung open.

"This is off limits," Garik pointed out. The off

limits didn't concern him. How Alyna was able to access it did.

"This isn't a spur-of-the-moment plan." Julia entered and pulled Garik after her.

"We're just being forced to move tonight." Alyna followed and closed the door after her.

"What's in here that we need?"

"An elevator directly to the parking garage. The labs have two."

"Oh." That was new information to Garik. The aboveground parking garage was where Kevin would have parked. He tried to picture the layout of the basement facility and place the parking garage outside the Tower over where he thought the research lab was located. It didn't fit. "I don't see how any elevators here could connect to the parking garage. It's behind the Tower. That's six blocks that way." He pointed behind them.

"We're headed to the underground garage."

"Okay." The two women didn't seem inclined to elaborate, and Garik let it go.

The research lab was massive, nearly a quarter of the size of the aboveground mall, and the corridor narrowed in the distance. A red exit light glowed in the distance. "That's us," Julia said.

Garik focused on the red light. He had no reason not to trust them, and a ton to do so.

At the elevator, Alyna inserted the passkey that had

granted them entrance into the labs. "One floor up. That's all we need. Come on, elevator."

The controls lit up, the door opened, and they stepped inside.

WHEN THE doors released them into the parking garage, Garik was the last one out. The vastness of the space confronting him contained as many parking spaces as he had ever seen in any one location, even more than Waldorf's Department Store, and their lot went for blocks. This was perhaps not larger, but it also didn't have a department store sitting in the middle of it.

Vehicles of different types filled about a third of the space, mostly small cars, several trucks, and some mini-vans. They were concentrated around the lab elevators and the main access that Garik reckoned sat directly under the tower. Numerous military vehicles filled the area to the left—the north wall, if Garik had his direc-tions down. From his early tours of the facility, he pic-tured the military housing block just to the west on the other side of the adjoining wall.

John, Laura, and Joanie stood to the right, with John wearing a backpack, and the two women sorting through several items at their feet. Farther away, Amy and Giselle walked side by side, Giselle rolling a large case, and Amy wearing a backpack. Marco scampered on four limbs beside them. John waved and called,

"About time. This way! Paolo and Leigh are on their way."

"And Justin?" Alyna yelled. Garik remembered her claws. He was certain she would return to the elevator if the news wasn't what she wanted.

"With Paolo and Leigh, we hope. They volunteered."

Garik didn't see Jantzen. What about the keys to Kevin's van? And if these people were all here, was this a mass exit, an escape of unimaginable proportions? He hadn't located Kevin's van, probably because there weren't any vans down here. If it was in the aboveground parking garage, how were they going to reach it?

And . . . and . . . when were they going to tell him *anything!*

Sheesh! It was as if he didn't count. He wanted to shout, "Hey! What's going on?" Instead, he picked up the pace and followed the others, wherever that might lead.

— 12 —

t first it seemed absurdly simple, that they might just walk out. Signs all along the ceiling directed them to the exit. How could they miss it?

It was the massive gate in the way that presented a problem. The passkey was their solution, or it should have been. Alyna pressed her thumb to the small screen on the side and slipped it into the access control panel. The panel turned on, telling her to validate the passkey with her palmprint.

It wasn't an option the hybrid escapees dared try.

Each person carrying one of the illegal passkeys

gave it a try, only to be kicked out like an unwanted child.

"Ideas?" Joanie sat on the floor, her back to the gate, and she pulled out a pack of mints. She popped two into her mouth before putting it away and didn't ask if anyone else was interested, a sure sign of her level of anxiety.

"If Leigh were here—" Giselle started.

"She's not." Joanie pulled out her pack of mints, shook it as if considering whether she should conserve, and decided to wait, putting the package away. Leigh could find invisible flaws, even accelerate chemical processes with her ultrasound, but she wasn't here, was she? "Alyna?"

The team knew the question exactly. Was Alyna prepared to slice through the locks, allowing them access to the parking garage above? They also understood the ramifications. As soon as the lock was severed, an alarm would sound, and their escape would be in dire peril.

Catch 22, no good way to find success through either option.

"I will, but we should exhaust our other choices, first. We will be pursued soon enough. No sense in starting the chase now."

John had the top of his backpack unzipped. He pulled out a watch with a blank, black face. He used his thumb to polish the glass surface.

"Tell me that works," Amy pleaded.

"Not in here." He looked up and around the room. "This place is a faraday cage. Only the project's electronics work underground, and only on their frequency. Once past this gate, I should have full-spectrum access to everything out there."

"Listen," Garik called out.

"What?" John's question was fair. It was the middle of the night. There had been no one coming or going out of the underground garage, and the sky they could just glimpse through the metal fretwork of the gate was black velvet littered with stars.

"You can't hear it?" Garik shook his head at the old people around him, their ears already gone.

"Garik's right." Amy stood, and she held perfectly still.

"At least Amy has ears," Garik muttered.

"She's not using her ears." Marco settled beside him, curling his tail into his lap and tugging on Garik's sleeve with a hand that had elongated, pawlike nails. "She's likely feeling the air pressure. Better than ears, sometimes."

"People moving this way," Amy said. "Julia, can you tell more?"

"No, not from this distance. Anyway, the concrete walls are difficult to work though." She had turned to face the direction of the elevators. They were a good three blocks away, if measured by the city above them.

"The other direction." Amy pointed through the gate.

Joanie turned, wrapped her fingers through the gate's openwork surface and pulled herself to her feet.

"Leigh?" she called, hissing the word.

"Joanie? Why isn't the gate open? We've located the van and are locked out. No keys."

"We hoped Jantzen would have them. Garik said—"

"Stop, Julia." Joanie held up a hand. "Unimportant. Software update. Locked in."

"Or out," Leigh said. "I can guide someone manually if anyone is willing to try to pick it."

"Or slice it," Alyna muttered, her claws on one hand already out and ready.

"Or pick it," Joanie reiterated, and she motioned with a hand for Alyna to be patient. "No alarm. Jantzen and Justin?"

"With us? Sort of, well, yes." Leigh wasn't saying everything.

"Okay. Understood. Marco, lock." Joanie's words were fully detailed to the people around her. Marco— part lemur adapted—had the smallest fingers in the group, and Leigh's ultrasound adaptation, allowing her to see what others couldn't, including the inner gearing of the gate's locking mechanism, were needed to get through the locked gate.

"Heh, heh, finally! Something I'm good at!" Marco scrambled over, wrapped his hands around the locking mechanism, sniffed of it, and smacked his lips. "Ready."

"Let me focus—"

As Leigh and Marco worked their magic, Joanie directed the others to gather their things. She pulled Garik aside, "Water?"

"In the backpack, sure. Do you need it?"

"Unsure. Be prepared." Joanie patted him on the shoulder and turned to see how the progress was going on the lock.

"It's hanging, Leigh. I am pulling. Can you get Paolo here? Hot water might work to expand parts of the metal." Marco growled at the lock.

"I can lubricate it, if you think that will help." Giselle offered her hand, her fingers already dripping.

"Try it," Leigh called. "It's almost there." The lock attached to a rotating assembly that interlocked in the center. It wasn't releasing enough to allow the gate to move.

Garik scanned the interlinked rods and the way they twisted together. He pictured his Street Strider and the gearing inside. He had rebuilt it on the side of the road enough times that he understood how to relieve the pressure on troublesome gears that liked to jump restrictive linkages.

"Here," he said. "Keep pulling that, Marco. I'll lift this here, and you, John, when I tell you, pull this rod towards you."

"That will help how?"

"Just do it!" Garik groaned in frustration. This was something he understood. They explained nothing to him. Then they expected him to explain everything to them. Sometimes things just needed done.

"Okay." John stepped to the gate, grabbed the rod, and said, "Ready."

Garik pulled, the rotating assembly moved, and he hissed, "Now, John."

With a snapping rotation that threw Marco backwards and startled Leigh, the locking mechanism released.

"We're through." Laura hefted a pack onto her shoulder just as alarms sounded, and strobe lights across the parking area flooded the space with midday brilliance.

Alyna groaned, "I could have done that," as she wrapped her arms around a box to carry to the other side.

"Now. Move." Joanie tugged on one gate, creating enough room for them to squeeze through. They were almost there. Just a little way to go.

JOHN SLIPPED through with a backpack on his shoulders, leading Laura. She held a zippered bag by the straps, and once through the gate, she took off running.

Marco squeezed past John, now in full run. He was on two feet this time, using his tail to balance the speed of his feet.

Leigh stood on the opposite side of the gate, helping people work their things through the tight opening. Amy, tiny Amy, had a backpack nearly her size. Her strength seemed inordinate to her stature, but she seemed to have no trouble.

Alyna had taken Garik's backpack of water bottles while he was helping with the gate, and she carried it and the box from earlier. He followed her through, both cutting into a run at the first opportunity.

Giselle's rolling case hung for a moment on the gate's tracks. Julia had one of Laura's bags in one hand, and she worked Giselle's case free with the other, helping her to get it rolling before they disappeared into the upper level.

Joanie was last, as any good leader should be, waiting on Leigh before putting her hand on the strap holding her backpack over one shoulder and making her way skyward.

At the van, they found Paolo hunched over Justin, who seemed a pale imitation of himself. Paolo looked overhead at the red lights flashing on the ceiling, running his eyes back and forth. Outside the garage, the night was black.

"Did anyone bring a key?"

"Where's Jantzen?" Joanie forced out two words, a good semblance of a complete sentence, revealing her desperation and determination to be understood.

"That's my sort of." Leigh knelt by the two men, and she asked Justin, "Can you hold on?"

"To you? Of course." He chuckled, laughed, and coughed blood.

Garik saw the complete picture. They were here. Jantzen was not. Whatever had happened to Justin, he needed to be someplace besides here. Alarms were going off, and there was no way they weren't going to be surrounded by the military in about two minutes. He was surprised they weren't already here.

They needed in the van, and he could get it started, even without a key.

Garik took Giselle's rolling case, and he said, "Excuse me, Giselle. Thank you." Lifting it, he smashed the bottom against the side glass. One wheel flew off, but when it came away, it left a crack. He smashed it again and again. "I'm sorry, Kevin," he said, as he hit it the fourth time, shattering the glass and sending the case tumbling inside. He reached through the door, felt for the lock, and slid the door open. He stood back and motioned for everyone to climb in.

"We still don't have the key," Paolo reminded him, as he stood and helped Justin stand.

"Leave that to me." As everyone began climbing into the van, Garik went around and opened the driver's door. He leaned under the dash and grabbed underneath the plastic housing enclosing the steering wheel and pulled until it broke free. "Sorry, again, Kevin," he said, and he tossed the plastic to the side. It clattered on the concrete floor of the garage. He began feeling for wires, certain he could bypass the ignition switch. He knew machines, had seen this done over and over in movies. How hard could it be?

"How long, Garik?" From Paolo. "We might need to make our exit."

"It should have an ignition lock switch I can bypass. I can't find it."

Something hit the outside of the van beside Garik's door, and he looked up to see Jantzen, bare-chested, standing over him, panting with exhaustion.

"What are you doing?"

"Hotwiring it, of course." Garik thought that was obvious. No key!

"And you broke the window for what reason?" Jantzen shook his head. "Giselle, I need some clothes out of that case."

She clicked it open, to the complaints of several others crowded in with her, and she handed him a set.

He began pulling on a pair of pants, and he called, "Giselle, the keys are in there, also. Hand them to me."

They appeared over the seat, and she dropped them into Jantzen's hand. He pulled his shirt on and motioned for Garik to get out of the way. He climbed in, started the van, and shifted it into gear.

"I told Kevin we wouldn't damage the van. He's not going to be happy. You should have used the key."

"I did."

Jantzen looked at him skeptically as he pulled the loaded van out of the parking garage and turned right onto Stamford. To the left, the serene residential lighting of the upscale properties in Overlook Estates seemed incongruous with the desperate escape happening in the van. Cold air poured in through the broken window.

"I did, I did," Garik insisted, turning to look at the faces behind him catching the lights along the street, flashing them into alternating patterns of light and dark. He grinned. "They just happened to still be in the case when I unlocked it."

They were barely more than a block away from Corona Mall, having just turned west on Corona and south on McKinley, when Corona Tower erupted with military vehicles streaming into the streets.

"I thought I could hold them longer." Jantzen put his foot to the floor, the engine in the transport van downshifted and began to roar, and it picked up speed. The passengers held on as Jantzen turned left on Paintbrush, then right on Park Avenue. With his foot planted, the van's speed soon surpassed anything the speed limit signs suggested as safe and legal.

Garik looked to the right as they passed the police station, lighted against the dark of night, and then it was gone.

Jantzen thought he could hold them longer. Garik

was sure he understood. The man had escaped his captors by evaporating into purple mist, and he had spent his time before arriving at the van jimmying all the exits to the building. He had bought them time for their escape.

They were on the run, and Garik didn't know exactly what that might involve, but if Jantzen was leading them, he had no doubts they would survive just fine.

"Jantzen, can we risk Bay City Medical?" Paolo's laidback voice filtered over the seat, only now, not so laid back.

"We are being pursued, Paolo." Very matter-of-fact.

"Just so you know, we're losing Justin."

Garik turned. Paolo held his hand on the man's chest. Blood seeped from between his fingers.

"John has a watch." Giselle pulled several items of cloth from the rolling bag, and she handed them to Paolo, saying, "Here, this should help temporarily."

"I've a better idea." Jantzen slammed the brakes and forced the van west, taking a hard right on Summit Court West. At the entrance to the Ransom Communications Building, he took a sudden left, skidding the tires just in front of a metal roll-up door.

"I'll be right back. Garik, can you pull us inside?"

"I can drive."

"Better than you can unlock a car?"

"Jantzen!" Garik wilted. "I didn't know the keys

were inside."

"I'll need my clothes." Jantzen grinned, balled a fist, and punched Garik on the arm. Then, he evaporated, leaving his clothes floating down to land on the seat.

"Move, boy," Joanie said, giving him a push on the shoulder.

As Garik shifted behind the wheel, purple smoke gathered around the roll-up door and disappeared through the gaps and cracks around the edges. Ten seconds later, the massive door began to roll upward.

Garik shifted into gear, and he eased the van forward.

He had no idea what he would find inside.

In Book Four, Garik reunites with his girlfriend, Marisa, and he learns the secret of the Silverback.

The Secret of the Silverback
Book Four
The Human-Hybrid Project

Garik Shayk is on the run from both the Human-Hybrid Project in the secretive sub-basements of the Corona Tower and the Tower's recovery teams determined to bring him back. Garik reunites with his girlfriend, Marisa Bruni, only to lose her once again when the Tower outwits and recaptures him. Does Garik decide to cooperate to regain his freedom, or does learning the secret of the Silverback convince him that cooperation is never an option?

The Human-Hybrid Project

Addictive!

A 10-book series you won't be able to forget. Explore each upcoming book, the characters, and more at www.thehumanhybridproject.com.

Book 1   Book 2

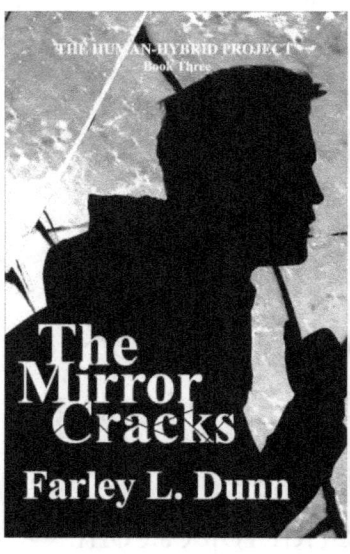

Book 3

Book 4

Book 5

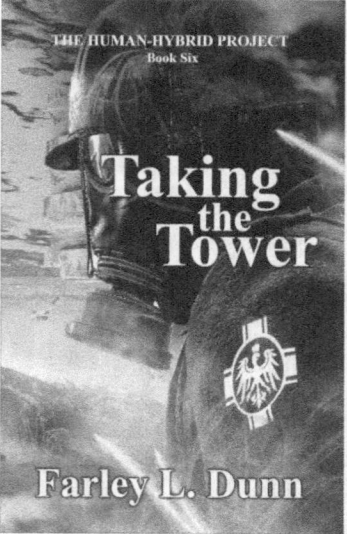

Book 6

Book 7   Book 8

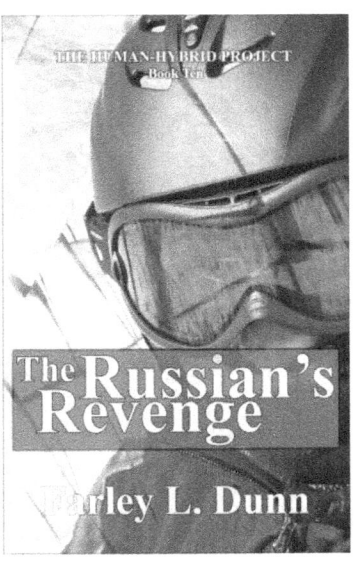

Book 9   Book 10

www.ingramcontent.com/pod-product-compliance
Lightning Source LLC
Chambersburg PA
CBHW070557180626
46817CB00005B/1879

* 9 7 8 1 9 4 3 1 8 9 9 3 9 *